Hostile
Takeover

By J.D. Bowen

MUCH LOVE!

JDB

Dedication

For Those We Have Lost:
Missy, Donne, and Lea Ellen

Acknowledgments

A very special thanks to the many people who had some kind of hand in the creation of this book: John M. Bowen, Sherrill Parker, Perry Bean, Greg Smith, Carter Smith, Michelle Nunez, Mac and Jane Bowen, and my proofreaders, Fay, Karen, Patrick, Ali, Carla and Herm, Sharlyn, Denise, Chet, Elaine, Gayla, and Jennifer.

CHAPTER 1

There seemed to be a million thoughts swirling around in her head and, oddly enough, she couldn't focus on any one thing. She closed her eyes and reflected on how she ended up in a cage and how she would function in the non-structured world outside after her release the next day. She had done eight years of a 15-year stretch for murdering her boyfriend, and this was the last night of her sentence; the last day of the only life Lydia Crane had known for eight years. Tomorrow would bring forth her rebirth. Her old identity would remain in prison, and her new self would set out on a mission to take what she figured the world owed her. During her incarceration, she had taken online business courses, earning a B.A. in Business and Marketing. She wasn't going to secure her fortune as a businesswoman, though, but by other means. The degree merely gave her enough knowledge to get her foot in the door. She knew she had to secure new passports and documents for identification, and she wasn't sure how that transaction would go, as she had never met the man who would provide them for her. Her cellmate and mentor had referred her to him. "It would be easy," she said to herself, because she knew if he gave her any trouble at all, she would have no problem killing him. Her boyfriend abused her on a daily basis, both physically and sexually. He was not unlike the same type of monster, disguised as her stepfather, that would creep into her room at night smelling of sweat, body odor, and gin, and ravage her young body, leaving her damaged and frightened. From the age of nine until she ran away at sixteen, she played the leading role in her own private horror movie. The emotional scars that were embedded in her psyche left her cradling an everlasting hatred for men. When abuse is served in small to medium-sized daily doses, only to be outdone by the frequent and horribly painful sessions that seem to transpire in slow motion, the systematic deconstruction of an otherwise normal personality is almost invisible to the naked eye. She had been slowly turned into a monster by the male gender. Since both of her tormentors were long dead, she focused her rage on the man who pounded the last nail in her prosecution: a man named Jon Archer, who took the stand and painted a picture of pure remorseless evil, saying that she should be put to death. The jury went from preparing to let her go to a cushy rehabilitation hospital to giving her 15 years in a maximum security prison, based solely on one man's testimony

The business con was only part of her plan, and it wasn't even the part that made her salivate. What really got her juices flowing was the sweet smell of revenge. As her eyes grew heavy while staring at the bumpy white painted bars that stood between her and her vengeance, she remembered a verse from Deuteronomy she had read in the prison Bible Study. She loved to argue the pros and cons of good and evil with the Christians. It went something like:

"Vengeance is mine said the Lord and I will repay. In due time their foot will slide. The day of disaster is at hand and doom will fall upon them."

She managed a wry smile and drifted off to sleep to the sound of her cellmate snoring in the bunk above her.

Her cellmate was cut from a different cloth altogether: she was more focused and clear about what she wanted and knew how to get it. Her name was Mavis T. McAvoy, but they called her "Rooster." They called her this because she was the cock of the walk, both on the outside and in the cellblock she called home at Metro State Women's Prison in Atlanta. She had a knack for finding out what someone wanted before she approached them in order to strike a deal, and she always had it ready to serve up. It was this type of business strategy that propelled her into the position called "The Storekeeper." Much like her vocation in the outside world, Rooster could get anything for any body, provided they could pay the freight, which was always heavily inflated. Cigarettes, booze, drugs, and candy, even sex: you name it and Rooster could get it because just like on the outside, she had contacts everywhere. This was the approach that Rooster taught to Lydia Crane. Everything that mattered in business came down to the preparations that had taken place before the negotiation, and Lydia now knew that. She not only knew how to prepare, but more importantly how to execute. It was this kind of knowledge that was going to aid her in her plan to make her fortune and guide her on her vengeful odyssey to finally cash in on the wages of sin.

Lydia was immediately drawn to Mavis, and the two of them became inseparable lovers. Mavis was the first and only person Lydia ever felt actual love for, and she was so amazed by the emotion that anything Mavis said was the gospel. They had been planning something very secret for the past several years that only they were privy to, and it was about to be set into motion

On the morning of her emancipation from the confines that had been both her tormentor and protector, she was calm. She spent the first few hours of the early morning in conference with Mavis. Huddled close together sitting on the bottom rack, whispering back and forth with deliberate caution, they plotted and schemed. The actual process of release was surprisingly fast. Following a shower and trading her jumpsuit for civilian clothes for the first time in 8 years, she went through a series of locked gates and eventually to the cage where she received a small manila envelope. It contained the personal effects she had upon arrival at the Fulton County lockup on Jefferson Street. There was a Polaroid picture of her stapled to the flap.

My God, I can't believe I ever looked like that.

She was shocked at the difference between the girl she was looking at and herself. The girl in the photo was emaciated with a hollow, sunken face, at least 40 lbs lighter with pink and black hair. She remembered that the deviant smile on the girl in the picture derived from knowing that this day inevitably would come. That same smile came across Lydia Crane's face for the second time. Then the Sergeant gave her an envelope with $73 inside, and she was led to an outside gate. As the deputy unlocked the gate, he wished her luck, to which she gave no response whatsoever and walked out.

CHAPTER 2

Jon Archer had two choices: get out of bed, drag himself to the shower, and make some kind of contribution to the world today, or roll over and sleep away all the symptoms of a colossal hangover. Since the Jack Daniels he drank last night was the culprit that turned his 6' 2" well defined frame into a weak, nauseous, muddled headed zombie, he chose the latter.

Twenty-five minutes later the phone rang. Several times. Through bloodshot eyes, he could see that the call was coming from his office. He knew it was his secretary, Mona Crumley, so he picked up the handset.

"Mona, there had better be a busload of orphans on fire," he groaned.

"Worse. Your Lieutenant Kincaid called from the Sheriff's Department; Lydia Crane is being released today. The deputy called from Metro last night. The Lieutenant said she tried to call you, but some drunken woman answered your cell phone and said you were on stage singing Willie Nelson?"

"Would you mind repeating that?"

"Lydia Crane is being released today," Mona said sharply.

There was a short pause. Then, in a coarse, raspy voice as he dropped the phone back on the receiver, he replied, "I think God hates me."

As he showered, he remembered feeling like he'd swallowed a brick the first time he met Lydia Crane. He had locked her up 8 years ago, and she was tucked safely away in Metro State Prison; or so he thought. She had murdered her boyfriend in a crystal meth-induced rage. Archer would never forget the homicidal look in her eyes when they snapped the cuffs on her to bring her in. Jon had the crime scene of Lester Doyle's apartment emblazoned in his brain. The living room looked like a blood bomb had exploded in it. The officer on the scene recorded Lydia's statements, and he remembered her saying that Lester was really the devil, and, if she could take off all of his skin, his true self would be revealed. She said that all men should be skinned so the world could see them for what they really were. The naked, skinless corpse of Lester Doyle was sitting on the couch, his hands and feet bound with the bailing wire that Lester sometimes used at work. The remote control was lashed to his hand and he was facing the TV like always. She had drugged him with enough barbiturates to incapacitate a rhino, and by the time he came to he was undressed and skinless from the waist down. He must have woke up a couple of times because there were bloody, broken liquor bottles all over the living room floor and big shards of colored glass sticking out of the top of Lester's skull. The Coroner said it probably took another 45 minutes for Lester to bleed out, plenty of time for Lydia to finish her grizzly task. As Archer stood dripping in a haze of steam from the shower, he shuddered as he thought about what Lester must have gone through in the final minutes of his life. He wasn't sure if he was cold or just abhorred the idea of crossing paths with Lydia Crane again.

As he drove his Range Rover down I-20 heading into Atlanta, his head was pounding. He had been born and raised in Georgia, and he lived about 50 miles east of Atlanta, part of the way between Atlanta and Augusta. His ranch was a fairly large spread with a couple of horses and a dog named Jimmy that had retired from active duty with the Army. His office was in Atlanta, at 1400 Colony Square Trace Midtown. He was the Owner and President of Archer Security, a firm that handled corporate security and body men for important clients who may need personal protection. Following graduation from West Point and a stint in the military, he served as a homicide detective for the Atlanta Police Department for 5 years. He had always excelled up the ranks wherever he was, largely because of his extremely high IQ, which had paid off more often than not in his security business. He still knew everyone at the station, and he used that when necessary. He normally enjoyed the commute to work. Driving through the country was usually therapy for him, but not today; Jack Daniels was working like a jackhammer on the inside of his skull. He couldn't remember ever feeling this bad before. "I need coffee," he mumbled to himself. He kept moving until he got off I-85 at Lenox Road, and when he pulled into his parking space he looked up at the rear view mirror. His forehead was beading with sweat, and he had black circles under his eyes. He felt as though his mind was playing tricks on him, and he had moments when vertigo would wash over him. He wiped his brow, slipped on his aviator Ray Bans, let out a long sigh, and exited his vehicle.

Archer's office building was a huge, 22-story structure that always reminded him of a gigantic cheese grater. The face of it had 22 rows of small windows stretching out across the front from top to bottom. Archer Security covered half of the seventeenth floor, and from his corner office he had a partial view of the downtown area to the South. He could also see north all the way to Marietta.

As Archer stepped off the elevator, he was greeted by Mona. Mona was a tough old bird, staunch, stern, and with her hair pulled to a tight, neat bun. She looked like an old schoolmarm. Her face reflected the worry and stress caused by working for and looking after Jon Archer for the last 30 years. She had worked for his father since he was a boy, then for him after his father died. Mona was as loyal as they come, but she always worried if Jon was eating right or sleeping enough, and he heard about it on a regular basis. She had a peculiar way of finishing her sentences with a question, like an old British woman would do. To the right of her desk was a block of cubicles with staff members watching monitors, talking on headsets, and coordinating communications with field agents on assignment. To her left was a long hallway with three senior agent offices. Archer's office sat in the corner. They jokingly called that side of the offices "Mahogany Row" due to the huge mahogany desks that resided in the offices of the senior agents. Across the hall there was a large Situation Room where all the planning was mapped out. It was also where Mona kept the coffee pot.

"Well now, we almost slept the day away, didn't we? Mona said with her arms crossed, holding a clipboard clutched to her chest.

"Doc's wife had a baby girl yesterday, so Brody and I met up with him at The Mug to celebrate."

Brody was Archer's right hand man, his champion. They met on a covert op in Bosnia during their time with Special Forces. They were in Sarajevo when the infamous call came in from Srebrenica for the French to send air support because they were under siege by a Colonel named Ratko Mladic, who was under the orders of a homicidal zealot named Slobodan Milosevic. He ordered his Serbian troops to wipe out the Muslim civilians, first by cutting off the food and water. Then they gathered 7500 men and boys and led them just out of sight – but not out of earshot – from their families, executing them by gunfire. It was clear to the world that the Serbian Army was committing genocide. That's when Brody came to the aid of an American reporter and navigated him through a war zone, protecting him from the onslaught of the Serbs and from Nato's return fire so he could make it out and let the word know what really happened there. They were both eventually arrested. The reporter won a Pulitzer Prize and Brody won Archer, since Archer was the one who had to break him out of a Bosnian detention center. They were the closest of friends ever since. Now Brody was a senior agent for Archer Security. Doc served as an MP and came to work for Archer when his hitch was over. Archer and Brody weren't as close to Doc as they were to each other. No one other than family members really got close to Doc, and he even kept them at a distance. It was a major social accomplishment for him to be able to come out and celebrate the birth of his daughter.

"I know all about the baby. Her name is Hanna, and that's no excuse for carousing around and drinking all night, is it?" said Mona.

"We were only going to have one toast until that woman, Keri, showed up."

"Ah, the mysterious drunken woman who answered your cell phone, hmm?"

"Yes, the Devil Incarnate herself," Archer mumbled.

Keri Martin was a party girl from the word go. Archer had not known her long. He met her at The Mug, and she took a shine to him right away. Most women did. Anytime she ran into him, she would try to shovel Jack Daniels into him by the glassful. It was her feeble attempt to get him in the sack. It had never worked before, and last night was no exception. Keri was excitable but seemed ok; she had a small body, her personality encompassed the epitome of white trash and she was always a mess. Bobby Mac, the bartender at The Mug, said she was a bit damaged. Apparently her son, Terry, was killed crossing the road after being let off the school bus. Keri did seem like a part of her was missing, and she always had that far away look in her eyes. Archer felt sorry for her, but it was always the same when she came around. She would start off the night drinking and laughing and having fun. Everything would be fine, then she would start thinking about how much she missed Terry, and by the end of the evening it was a sad display of heartache and tears. It suddenly occurred to

Archer that he didn't remember the drama fest from last night. In fact, he didn't remember anything at all from the time Brody drove the guys home until this morning. He certainly did not remember singing Willie Nelson.

'Mona, will you get Lieutenant Kincaid on the phone for me please?"

"Right away, Jon…you fancy her a bit, don't you?" Mona replied.

Archer knew Mona was right. Jane Kincaid was as sharp as a razor and utterly intoxicating. She had hair the color of sunshine and smoky green eyes. They had been out a few times, and Archer was smitten. Back in his APD days, she was a rookie when he was a lieutenant in Homicide. They knew each other vaguely, and he remembered always thinking she was the kind of beautiful woman a guy could get lost in.

Archer stopped by the Sit Room to get coffee, and as he poured a ridiculous amount of sugar in it, it hit him. Edelman from the D.A.'s office must have not showed up at Lydia's parole hearing. Everyone knew that Clarence Edelman hated Archer. He had tried to get Archer to testify at the trial of a kid who had been arrested for attacking a woman outside the Dome at a Falcons game. Edelman wanted Archer to swear, under oath, that he saw the kid following the woman to her car parked in the Green Lot, when, in fact, Archer had seen the kid, but in the Gold Lot, selling Cokes to tailgaters out of a cooler full of ice in a wagon he was dragging behind him. The kid was a thirteen year-old, a skinny boy who weighed about 85 pounds soaking wet, who probably couldn't have taken the woman if he had brass knuckles. When

Archer refused to testify against him, Edelman lost and said he wouldn't forget what Archer had done. So, by conveniently forgetting Lydia Crane's parole hearing date, it was his chance to poke Archer in the eye with a sharp stick. It was no skin off of Edelman's back; he got the conviction 8 years ago, and he smiled widely when he heard Lydia Crane swear revenge on Archer in open court.

Archer stewed as he walked into his office muttering under his breath about what he really thought of Clarence Edelman. Just then the phone buzzed. Mona had Lieutenant Kincaid on line one.

"Good morning, Jane," Archer said.

"Hello Archer. How you feeling today?"

"I've been better."

"You must have really tied one on. Sounds like you were having a good ole time. Who was the secretary last night?"

"Keri Martin must have grabbed my phone off the table. Do I detect a hint of jealousy?"

"I know you too well; you're far too much of a gentleman to take advantage of someone that drunk. Are you alright?"

"Not really, I only had a few; I don't know why I feel so bad."

"Maybe someone slipped you something."

For some reason, that thought had never even occurred to Archer.

"Maybe I'll go see the doctor. But here's the most important thing: how did Lydia Crane get out of prison so soon?"

"Not sure. Well, let's see, she served just under two thirds of a fifteen-year hump, good behavior and no objections at the parole hearing. I could see that happening."

"Yeah, about that Jane. Where was Edelman?"

"Two weeks vacation."

"That's no coincidence."

"Knowing how he feels about you, I would bet my bottom dollar it's not."

"Did they give any indication as to when they were letting her go?"

"Not really. The deputy did say sometime before lunch."

"OK. Hey, any plans for the weekend?"

"My only plans were to have no plans at all: in other words do absolutely nothing"

"Would you like to come out to the ranch and do nothing with me?"

"It's a date. I'll swing by my place and grab an overnight bag and see you there around 6:30."

"Great, I can stop by the Farmer's Market on the way home and pick up some groceries. Thanks for the heads up on Lydia."

"Anytime, Handsome."

Archer didn't even hang the phone up. He punched another line and hit speed dial for Brody.

"Brody?"

"Yeah, Boss?"

"Get a Doc over to Metro Prison and put a tail on Lydia Crane. She's being released today. If she's already gone when he gets there, have him check around at the motels in the area."

"I'm on it."

As he hung up the phone, he noticed he was feeling very dizzy and his vision was blurred. He buzzed Mona.

"Yes, Jon?"

"Mona, see if Doctor Stevens can see me now."

"Right away. Are you alright? Can I get you anything?….. Jon……Jon?"

When Archer woke up, he was lying on the suede couch in his office with Doctor Stevens standing over him. He was a kindly, old southern doctor who had an office on the third floor. Jon had used him for the last few years after his family physician passed away.

"Mona, make sure he gets a lot of rest this weekend. I've taken a blood sample and given him a shot of B12. Whatever's the matter with him, we'll know soon enough, but for now it seems to be passing."

"Yes, Doctor. Goodbye and thank you," answered Mona.

"What happened?" asked Archer.

"You passed out right after asking me to call Doctor Stevens. Are you OK to drive home?"

"Yes, I actually feel alot better."

"That's the B12. Works wonders, doesn't it?" replied Mona. "Do you think you may have picked up something from somebody?"

"I don't know, but I have an idea. Thanks, Mona."

"You rest yourself Jon Archer, and I'll come by the ranch tomorrow with some soup."

"That's alright, Mona, Jane is spending the weekend at the ranch. She can nurse me back to health," Archer replied, walking to the elevator.

"Wonderful. You will try and hang onto this one, won't you?"

"With both hands, Mona, with both hands."

CHAPTER 3

The July sun was high and hot, and the air looked wavy as she looked down Constitution Road toward Moreland Ave. There was a shuffle of feet behind her from three more women following her down the walk to the road where the prison bus was waiting, manila envelopes in hand. The bus smelled like a combination of sweat and oil, and in some places the floor was rusted through, displaying the road rushing under your feet. It was an old Bluebird bus that was once used to carry children to a place of academia; now it was used to ferry the dregs of man, who had supposedly paid their debt to society, to rejoin the general population. Whether it was sweet justice or tragic irony, it made no difference to Lydia. All she knew was it was her chariot of salvation, taking her to the promised land of wealth and re- venge.

The prison bus took them as far as the Grey- hound Station on Forsyth Street. She chuckled at the less than subtle attempt to dispatch the ex-cons to another state. They would drop them off right in front of the terminal where big pictures hung of far away places like New York, Florida, and New Orleans, and with a little money in their pockets and the promise of a new life they almost ran to the ticket counter. Lydia Crane had other plans.

She walked through the terminal and stopped briefly in front of a numbered locker where she inserted the key Mavis had given her and took out the package. Then she exited the other side looking over her shoulder, making sure she was not followed. Mavis had warned her to be careful in case the cops were keeping an eye on her, and she didn't want to drag a tail to the meeting where she was to pick up her papers. A few weeks earlier, Mavis had written down all of Lydia's information: age, weight, height – the rest she invented. She had a guard mail it to her contact from a mail center outside the prison.

Lydia took a Marta Bus over to Jones Ave and got off across the street from Mom's Soul Food Restaurant. It was one thirty, and her meeting was at two. She decided to go in and eat before he arrived. The moment the screen door slammed shut behind her, she knew she was out of place. Not only was she was the only white person in the place, but she was the only woman in the place, besides the old fat woman behind the counter turning pork chops over in a huge skillet of popping grease. There was a juke box in the corner crying out a Percy Sledge song as a layer of smoke rolled across the ceiling. Just above the door there was an autographed picture of Hosea Williams. Two old men sat in the corner playing cards, spitting in a shared cup full of brown, wet paper towels, and there was a guy sitting at the counter scratching off a long strand of lottery tickets. Aside from the smell of stale cigar smoke, the aroma of the pork chops frying smelled pretty good to Lydia. She ordered a pork chop sandwich that was served in a Styrofoam box.

The pork chop still had the bone in it and was between two slices of white bread. On the side were fried corn and collard greens that had a big chunk of ham hoc sticking out of it. The meal, with a glass of sweet tea, came to $4.50. She laid six dollars on the counter and retreated to the back where there was a card table and two chairs. She sat and ate with her back to wall while watching the door; the food tasted terrific since she hadn't had anything but prison food in years. She ate quickly, not realizing she had her arms on either side of the box of food like she did in prison to protect what was hers. When she had finished, she discarded her empty box in the 55 gallon drum used for a garbage can and returned to the table and her iced tea. It was already past two, and nothing. She was getting impatient. Just as she was about to leave, a skinny black kid came though the door wearing a "Tupac Forever" t-shirt and a Braves hat. He looked around sheepishly and made eye contact with Lydia.

His name was Harlan Robinson; he claimed he was a distant cousin of Smokey Robinson. If he wasn't, he could have been. Harlan would go down to a blues joint called Blind Willie's and sit in some nights and play slide guitar and had a voice as sweet as Smokey himself. He wasn't a bad guy; he was just dealt a bad hand. He was poor and had no skills other than forging documents and the money he made selling a few drugs only went to support his own habit. He didn't consider music a skill; it was more like a spiritual thing for him. In Harlan's mind, taking money for playing music was somehow a sin. He always thought he was one move away from freeing himself from his oppressive life. His mother had died when he was a baby and his father worked in the scrap yard downtown for thirty years until he had a stroke; now he just sat on the porch all day and waved at every car that passed. The government pays for most of his medication and they survive on whatever money Harlan can keep from spending on Black Tar Heroin and actually bring home. He was always broke and always late paying his bills. Harlan took it upon himself to learn the fine art of forgery when a friend of his called Snapshot started losing his sight and it affected his work. Snapshot was a photographer for the DMV by day and a forger at night. He taught Harlan everything he knew, and with the advancements and availability of home computer systems and laser printers, Harlan took it to a new level.

"Harlan!" shouted the lady from behind the counter

He spun his head around and saw her.

"Hey, Moms," he said cheerfully.

"Don't you 'hey, Moms' me – you ain't paid your food ticket for last week," she bellowed.

"I know, I know, I get paid today. I promise I'll bring it to you."

"Promises don't pay shit; I'll fry your ass in my skillet if you don't have my money tomorrow."

"Yes, Ma'am, I'll bring it to you. I promise, I mean…I will." Harlan stammered.

He shoved his hands in his pockets, dropped his head and started towards the back.

Harlan sat down across from Lydia Crane. "I recognized you from your picture. How's Rooster doing?"

"She's getting out soon and she said not to take any shit from your dumb ass. You got something for me?" snapped Lydia.

"Yeah, Goddamn. I have it out in my truck," Harlan said looking around nervously. He was clearly high, and he kept closing his eyes for a few seconds at a time.

"Harlan, you nodding like this is making me a little nervous. Look at your eyes, man."
"I ain't done much of that Jack today. I'm just tired," he said as he started scraping the label off of a bottle of Tabasco sauce with his fingernail.

"How about I take a little crystal off your hands," asked Lydia.

"Look, Rooster told me not to get you anything if you asked."

Remembering her training from Mavis in the art of negotiations, she knew what Harlan wanted by the way he was looking her up and down.

"Well what Mavis doesn't know won't hurt her, will it? Look, the papers are $500 right? I'll give you another hundred, and I'll make the rest up to you out in your truck for an eight ball," Lydia said with a wink.

Harlan's eyes lit up and he looked a little embarrassed and like he was going to burst, "Let's go."

Walking back to the bus stop after servicing

Harlan, she felt no shame at all. It wasn't the first time she had used sex to get what she needed. It was just the first time she'd done it with a man in a few years. He served as a means to an end. She was going to find a hotel, inspect her package and new papers, and get intimate with the demon that had been off her dance card for 8 years. Harlan went back inside Mom's and paid her for his meal tickets, then whistled all the way home.

CHAPTER 4

    Archer drove out of the parking structure at Colony Square and realized he needed food. He headed down Peachtree Street toward 14th and jumped on the 75/85 connector via Techwood heading south to North Ave. His favorite place for food downtown was The Varsity. The Varsity was a drive-in restaurant that had three floors of indoor seating as well, and it was famous for chili dogs and home made onion rings. The place went through three hundred gallons of chili a day. It was built in 1928 by Frank Gordy for $2000 right across the street from the Georgia Tech campus. Saturdays during football season, when the Jackets were playing in town, they would serve 30,000 people in one day, and obviously you couldn't get a seat in the place. It was widely considered to be the World's Largest Drive Thru.

    He swung into the curb service parking and rolled down his window. A few seconds later he was approached by an old man named Shorty asking "What'll you have, Mr. Archer," with a wide smile.

"A chili dog and Varsity Orange please, Shorty," replied Archer. Archer never went inside; he always used the curb service. Shorty usually took care of him when he came in, but his favorite was always Flossie Mae. He would sing and dance the menu to the delight of young children and worked that lot for over 50 years. Nipsey Russell got his start working the lot at the Varsity.

"Coming right up, Mr. Archer."

Ten minutes later he was heading out 1-20 on his way back home, chewing on a chili dog and feeling better. He stopped off at Harry's Farmer's Market and picked up a couple of ribeyes and potatoes and some other stuff, as well as a bag of dog food for Jimmy. Driving home through the country was clearing his head. He began to question whether Keri Martin or anyone else could have slipped him a mickey, which would explain him not remembering anything and causing him to pass out.

But why?

About ten miles off the highway, not far from Archer's place past Hodgens Lake down a winding dirt driveway, covered with thick oaks lining both sides, lived a man named Odean Bass. He was an old black man who had lived on and worked that land for 75 years. His wife died some 30-odd years ago, and he lived alone. He had a son who lived in New York and worked on Wall Street and visited him on holidays. Archer had known him his whole life. Odean used to be friends with Archer's father, and when Archer was a boy he used to visit him, and Odean would tell his fortune. Odean was a self proclaimed prophet. He always used to say God put him here to warn other people when things were wrong. He knew things no one else did. Once, when Archer was in high school, a little 11 year-old girl named Laney Henderson went missing. The whole church searched all day and night, and when they came up empty the sheriff drove out to see Odean. Odean told the sheriff he had a dream that a little girl was carried off by a red fox. They rode around the Southeast part of the county in the sheriff's truck, and Odean kept his eyes closed the whole time, telling the sheriff when to turn and which way. They did this for over an hour until they came to Meed Quarry. Laney Henderson was found on the edge of the quarry lying limp in the big rocks. She had been beaten, sexually assaulted, and left for dead. Her bruised, swollen face had been cooked in the hot Georgia sun, and she had terrible sun blisters covering her tiny little legs. After a week in the hospital, little Laney came to and told the deputies that a big man with red hair and a bushy beard driving a big blue shiny car took her when she was walking home from her neighbor's house. She described him as sweaty and smelling like beer. Two days later, they arrested the guy in a pool hall in Thomaston. He fit the description of the guy and he had a rap sheet that spanned over three counties with countless arrests for lewd and lascivious behavior. Laney picked him out of a mug shot line up. Laney's parents didn't even bother to thank Odean. They, like many others, were afraid of what they thought Odean was. They whispered and pointed at him when he would come to town, which was infrequent since Odean raised his own food and livestock. He hardly got out at all these days, so Archer would bring him some tobacco and a couple of bottles of wine from time to time.

Archer was driving slowly under the flicker of lights shooting down from the oaks to the worn, sun-bleached home of Odean Bass. When Archer reached the house, Odean, who was wearing coveralls and a straw sun hat and mopping his brow with a bandana, was working on the engine of a small tractor that looked to be about as old as he was. Odean shuffled past Archer's truck and grumbled "C'mon" and never even looked at him. Archer fell in tow, holding his grocery sack and following him into the kitchen. Odean opened the refrigerator and pulled out a glass orange juice bottle full of sweet tea. He swiped two cups off the shelf and started walking back out, leaving the refrigerator open. "Put that what ya got there in the icebox. I like it cold, 'cept for the tobacca. You did bring tobacca didn't you?" he said as he stopped and looked up widely at Archer waiting for an answer.

"Yes, sir, of course I brought you some."

"Well, all right then," he said turning back around content and walking out. Archer put the bottles away and followed him back outside. Odean was dipping cracklins out of a big iron pot hanging over a fire in the pit behind his house and dumped them in some paper towels he had torn off the roll. He shook a large shaker full of salt, seasoned salt, and black pepper over the cracklins and came over to the picnic table under a persimmon tree and poured them each a glass of tea putting the grease-soaked paper towel between them. He pulled a bottle of Tabasco out of his coveralls and poured it over the cracklins.

"I knew you was coming today. I had one of my dreams last night. Did you know you has trouble coming?" he said, looking up with one eye shut and spitting a hard cracklin out of the side of his mouth. Just then a breeze blew through the persimmon tree, setting off an orchestra of chimes from a group of colored, emptied bottles hanging from twine from the branches. Odean believed they were supposed to ward off evil from his property.

"No. maybe I just haven't been by in a couple weeks, and I wanted to see you," Archer said, trying his best to look sincere.

"Boy, you ought to go on away from here," Odean said, cackling with laughter. "You tell a lie when the truth fits better."

"Well, alright, maybe I thought it was getting a little cloudy. I just wanted a weather report."

Odean put his glass of tea down and looked Archer square in the eye. In a low whisper he said, "A storm's coming your way, Boy. A storm you ain't ready for."

"Tell me about this dream," Archer asked, listening intently.

"There was a great big mountain you were trying real hard to climb. A mountain so high you couldn't see the top of it and there was witches chasing you and these witches was traveling with a jackal. He kept running ahead of you, putting trouble in your path."

"What was on the mountain that I wanted so badly?"

"A yellow-haired angel. You needed her to stop the witches. A woman that fine ain't nothing but trouble. In fact, you need to stay away from the

Angel, the witches and that mountain. You need to go home and plant that back pasture you got," Odean said, finishing his lunch.

"Well, when I do I'm coming to get you to help me. No one knows the soil around here better than you do, Odean. You know that."

Archer stayed a while and helped Odean load up bushels of speckled butterbeans he had picked to be sold. The local vendors that sold vegetables and rattlesnake watermelons on the side of the road would come by and purchase them.

Archer said goodbye and thanked Odean for the warning, even though he wasn't really sure what he had just been warned about.

As he crossed onto his dirt driveway, the rumble of the cattle guard was like a starting pistol. Jimmy came barreling out from under the oak tree where he was having his afternoon nap and caught up to the truck. Racing alongside the truck as Archer jammed the gas, the race was on. The first hundred yards, Jimmy was nose and nose with the truck, but as the last hundred yards trudged by he started falling back. Jimmy was a Boxer and was starting to get old, and he couldn't split the wind quite like he used to. Archer eased back off the accelerator and let Jimmy catch up and even pull ahead a little. When they reached the house, Jimmy was clearly the victor, and he was pretty proud of himself as he paced back and forth on the sidewalk leading up to the front door with his head held high. Archer carried the groceries to the house and praised Jimmy for his valiant effort, then punched in the alarm code. When he opened the door, Jimmy was already inside using the doggie door and still feeling quite clever. He fed Jimmy and quickly made a marinade for the meat. He submerged the steaks for dinner and went to have another shower to wash the sweat off, and, with a fresh pair of jeans and a T-shirt, he was staring to feel like his normal self again. He went downstairs, put in a Robert Johnson CD, and played "Hell Hounds on My Trail" as a victory song for Jimmy.

Archer bought this place when the owner, his uncle, Silas Archer, got too old to keep it up and moved to a retirement home in Conyers. Archer lived on the ranch with Silas and Miss Virginia back when they still had cattle, before the boll weevils took the cotton they had in the back. Silas and his wife, Miss Virginia, lived there for over 50 years. They absolutely adored each other. It was one of the great love affairs on this earth, and when she passed away about 15 years ago, on her deathbed she swore to Silas that she would come back and look after him and the ranch. Silas was never the same after she was gone. He would sit and stare at her chair in the front room and sometimes talk to her. He used to say that dying would be easy, because the only thing he was living for was Miss Virginia. After she had gone, Silas was too heartbroken to be of much good to himself or anyone else. Long are the hours and many are the hard days that befall the heartbroken. Losing his love had most certainly broken Silas Archer. One trip when Archer came home on leave from the Army, Uncle Silas asked him to buy the place for just enough money to buy him a bed at the home so he could die. Uncle Silas had plenty of money, he just liked the idea of doing business or he had forgotten about the drum full of money buried on the ranch. When he first came back home to stay, Archer used to call Uncle Silas at the retirement home and say that things would be put away that he had left out, or that he thought things were missing, and Silas would tell him that it was just Miss Virginia tidying up. Jimmy would stop beside her chair in front of the fireplace where Miss Virginia used to sit and lower his head while wagging his tail as if someone was petting him. Sometimes it was just downright spooky at night when they would hear noises. And often, if the wind was blowing, Archer would swear he heard the faint sound of a woman singing "Down By The Riverside," which was Miss Virginia's favorite song. One night when Brody had come over to talk about a job they were on, he was leaving and he said something snatched him back by his collar just as a piece of soffit board fell down from the overhang on the front porch, shattering on the brick steps where he would have been. Now Brody won't go near the house unless Archer is there. He parks up by the big oak tree at the front of the property and waits with Jimmy.

Archer had a surveillance system and a panic room installed well after he bought the place from Silas. The kind of business he was in warranted such an expense, especially after what happened to his girlfriend. After hearing that Lydia Crane was sprung,, he's glad he did. With the gun safes, cameras, steel doors, and security windows, his place was a fortress.

Archer was excited at the idea of Jane coming for the weekend; he started cutting the lettuce he had washed into quarters for iceberg wedge salads. He crumbled some Maytag bleu cheese and put it all in the refrigerator to chill. The oven was preheated now, so he rolled the potatoes in foil and put them in. Archer fixed a glass of iced tea that he had been steeping and went out to the back porch. Walking out through the sliding glass (bulletproof) doors, he could see the rolling pastures behind the house. The lush, green grass seemed to be frosted at the tips with gold from the afternoon sun. He could smell the honey-suckle vines growing along the fence to the garden on his left. The background was filled with life; cotton-tails scampered back and forth and deer were starting to come out of the tree line and make the long, exposed trek across the pasture. He could smell the sweet cherry tomato plants from the garden. It reminded him to turn the sprinklers on; he had already picked a small bowl that they would have with supper. An old black man named Luscious came by once a week to tend to the garden. All Archer had to do was remember to turn the water on, which he hardly ever failed to do. Luscious would bring his wife, Alice Mae to come clean the house and wash clothes for Archer. They sort of came with the house. They worked for Uncle Silas for as long as Archer could remember. He used to go pick them up and take them home every week. Two years ago, Archer bought them a brand new Aerostar van. They had 6 children and 11 grandchildren, so they needed the extra space.

Jimmy suddenly left his side and ran to the front room and put his paws up on the couch in front of the big glass picture window and gave a low growl. The natural grain of his coat met between his shoulders and crested high when he was in warning mode. He pointed with his nose and held the constant growl until Archer came to his side.

"Whadda ya got, Killer?"

CHAPTER 5

Lydia Crane got out of a cab in front of the Super 8 Motel by the World Congress Center in Downtown Atlanta, went inside, and checked in. In her room, she turned on the air conditioner and sat down at the little desk. She dumped the contents of her package and the envelope she had gotten from Harlan out and started looking through the various papers. There was her Social Security card, credit cards, and a birth certificate from New Jersey. There also was a framed Masters Degree in Economics from Princeton and a 9mm with 2 extra clips and some cash. There were a few newspaper clippings and magazine articles with a man's picture on them circled in red marker; he was the mark. Other items included a cell phone and the business card of a Dr. Van Landingham. She took out the letter that Mavis had given her; she had said to open it once she had the package.

Lydia,

The contents of this package should be what you need to proceed. I've had a computer hacker I know do all the work to back up these documents. The credit cards work and have a $10,000 limit on each. The Drivers License is a paper one so you have to go down to the DMV and get a picture taken after you see the Doc. You have a history of speeding. I couldn't resist the irony. The passport paperwork is sent in so just go there for a picture too. The degree is real, as far as Princeton knows anyway; you're in their database. Information and bios of the mark are included. He plays racquetball every Monday and Friday at the Peachtree Center Athletic Club at 5pm and goes down to a place on the street level called Gibney's Pub and has martinis 'til about 7pm. If for some reason you need the muscle earlier, there is a phone number programmed in your cell phone for a guy named Mac. You have an appointment with a plastic surgeon on Monday. His card is in the package and it's all been taken care of. You know what to do from here. Good luck and remember: Lydia Crane is now dead. You are Darla Davis. I'll see you soon, and dream of when we can be together again.
M

Darla immediately wrapped everything back up in the package and opened up the knotted cellophane bag that she had gotten from Harlan. She used the motel key to shovel a pile of crystal meth in her nostril as she snorted hard. The blast rushing up the side of her head burned like it was Drano as every pore on her body seemed to ooze energy. It made her left eye pour with tears. She gathered herself and left the motel without bothering to check out. She hailed a cab and took it to the Marriott Marquis on Courtland

Street, right across the street from Gibney's. She rented a suite and again turned up the air. Controls to an air conditioner were a luxury she hadn't had for a long time. She removed the newspaper and magazine articles from the package and spread them out on the bed. She opened the wide, wall-size curtains to a spectacular view of Atlanta. She called room service and ordered a bottle of Tanqueray gin, some limes, and a club sandwich and began to read. Throughout the rest of the evening, Darla Davis read everything she had on Thomas Reynolds. This would be easy no matter what kind of man he was. He was still a man who would take what he wanted, whether it was consensual or not; therefore he deserved to die.

He needs to be skinned!

She went down to the business center in the lobby and Googled him, finding a treasure trove of information. Thomas Reynolds was a very industrious man. He started a business called Reynolds Press when he was 18; from there it grew on a steady incline. He now was the founding partner in Reynolds Enterprises, one of the largest media corporations in the country. They owned hundreds of radio and TV stations, newspapers and magazines and every kind of media venue you could imagine, right down to 50,000 billboards. He was a long standing member of The Atlanta Chamber of Commerce and a staple in the community.

Skinned!

She finally passed out and dreamed of mansions and riches beyond her wildest imagination, where her bidding was done the instant she commanded.

CHAPTER 6

Archer looked out the front window and saw Jane's car moving up to the house.

"Jimmy, guard," Archer said in a playful voice.

Jimmy raced through the doggie door and was on the hood of Jane's car almost before she could put it in park. In guard mode and staring straight through the windshield warning with a constant growl, Jimmy looked directly into her eyes. Archer rushed outside.

"Jimmy down. Jane's a friend!" commanded Jon.

"Thanks, Tarzan," replied Jane as she slowly got out of her car.

"It's alright now, you're safe Ma'am. He's a little protective."

"Yeah, you probably ordered him to sic me," she said, only half smiling.

Immediately Jimmy lowered his head and while wagging his tail approached Jane and administered kisses. Jane went down to one knee, scratching Jimmy behind the ears with both hands. He rolled over drawing the attention to his belly and from that moment on they were great friends.

Archer heard the phone ring inside.

"Come on in, I'll get your bag" he said.

"Don't be silly, I'm a big girl….go….go."

"Alright," Archer chuckled. "I'll just be a minute. Make yourself at home, pretty lady. There's sangria in the refrigerator."

Ironically enough, when Jane walked in the kitchen towards the fridge, she heard Robert Johnson singing "Come on in My Kitchen." She looked at Jimmy, who tilted his head curiously.

Archer ran into the foyer and to the left where his study was and grabbed the phone.

"Hello," Archer answered.

"Hi, Boss."

"Howdy partner. Any news?"

"A little, but nothing to get a boner over. We missed her at Metro. She had already been released. I interviewed the prison bus driver, and he said she went into the terminal with the rest of them, and then he left. We narrowed down what time that was, and we borrowed a little satellite time from one of our clients who shall remain nameless and watched her go in, wait a few seconds, and come out the opposite door looking behind her to see if she was being followed. She hopped a Marta bus that drove northeast, off the grid. I had Doc check out all the motels. He got a hit at the Downtown Super 8, but the man at the desk, a Nick Patel, said she got in a cab 10 minutes after she got there, bags in hand. She's still gone, and the room's empty. She's AWOL"

Doc was the man you put on a job like that. He was a man of few words and even fewer opinions. He was competent and methodical and a great field man; relentless.

"OK, run a camera sweep. ATMs, store surveillance and traffic cams, around the motel, try and get a taxi number. If you can, interview the driver. We can assume that since she's gone and the room's empty, then she's not coming back. All ex-cons have a small amount of personal belongings and when that's all you have then you tend to keep it close. Then review the security cams at the bus terminal. I want to know why she hesitated in the terminal before re-emerging." What the hell is she up to? "Also, have Doc check all the hotels now, if we're right about her not coming back, then she either has someone putting her up, or she got her hands on some money – and Lydia Crane doesn't exactly strike me as having a lot of friends."

"Roger that, we'll stay on it until something shakes out. You bunkered down for the weekend?" asked Brody.

'Yeah, Jane Kincaid's here."

"You lucky bastard."

"I attribute it to clean living, but luck doesn't hurt either"

"Right, I'll call you with any news. Otherwise see you at the office on Monday. You should come dressed to fish. I want to have a spoon in the drink before dark, savvy?"

"You're such a redneck," Archer said, then hung up.

He joined Jane and Jimmy in the kitchen. She was taking the potatoes out of the oven and she caught him staring at her from behind. Her long, sunshine blonde hair was spilling down her back, and Archer felt a twinge in his loins. They hurried through a fine steak dinner and some sangria. Unable to stop staring at each other, and smiling all the time, they eventually retired to the bedroom. She went into the bathroom, and Archer undressed and got in bed. When she emerged, she was wearing only a T-back. Her body was perfection. Toned and tan with a flat stomach and ample breasts, she stripped them off and climbed in with him. Her body was soft and warm. She climbed on top and inserted him inside her. She began to rise and fall in a rhythmic motion and toss her hair around like she was on one of those mechanical bulls. After almost an hour, they both arrived at Happy Land at the same time and fell back side-by-side, panting and sweating. They were asleep in minutes.

The next morning, Archer awoke to the smell of coffee and bacon. Jane was already showered and was downstairs cooking breakfast.

He took a leisurely shower and went down himself to join her.

"Good morning, Handsome," Jane said in a flirty little voice. "I slept like a baby. I kept thinking I was hearing singing. I think it was that old song 'Down By The Riverside?' "

Miss Virginia?

Archer tried to explain about Miss Virginia, but it was useless. She was convinced he was playing with her and thought it was cute that he would make up such an elaborate story to entertain her.

After breakfast, Archer turned the stalls and saddled up the horses, Frank and Jesse, and they rode the fence line of the property, Jimmy in tow. He found a spot where the grass was matted, just down the gully from the house. Normally, Archer would have chalked this up to deer bedding down, but there were 2 cigarette butts crushed on the ground. He stood in the middle of the depression and looked back towards the house. He could see directly into his breakfast room right through the sliding glass door.

"What do you make of that?" he asked.

"I think you're being watched," replied Jane.

"I'd have to agree."

"There are no tracks from tires or hooves, so they would have had to hike in," Jane pointed out.

"I think the cameras on my back porch might capture this spot. I'll review the files and see if we get anything. Watch this," Archer said proudly.

He knelt down and patted the ground in the depression.

"Jimmy, pick it up" Archer said sternly.

On cue, Jimmy started sniffing the area in a grid like pattern and sat down looking at Archer.

"Find 'em, boy" Archer commanded.

Jimmy darted up the fence line, which was under the cover of shade because the fence line was also the tree line. Thick cypress trees formed a wall of green just behind the fence. They followed behind Jimmy on horseback until he led them past the big oak tree and off the property. There they found another cigarette butt and some tire tracks from a small car on the road. Archer dismounted and knelt down by the tire tracks and felt the ground palm down. Then he picked up some of the dirt out of the track and smelled it. He looked to see if Jane was watching him.

"Come on, Geronimo, let's go," Jane said, rolling her eyes and laughing.

They ambled back to the house and had a steak sandwich lunch from last night's leftovers on the back porch.

After lunch, Archer went to his study to review the video files on his computer, then called Brody.

"Hey, Boss," Brody answered.

"I think Lydia Crane was here last night. Jane and I went for a ride out behind the house, and I found some evidence of someone watching the place. So, I checked the video and saw the shape of someone small, like a woman. I didn't get a good look because it was dark, and they were in the shadows. I'll be ready if they come back tonight," Archer said.

"Anything you want me to do, want me to bird dog her?" asked Brody.

"No, but make sure we have field people on staff for next week. I want my house on watch. If anybody fucks around out here while we're out of town I want it to be covered. As far as the rest of the weekend, I have a lovely Police Lieutenant to look after me," quipped Archer.

"Call if you need the cavalry. Otherwise I'll see you at the office on Monday, and we'll head for the hills and be stinky for a week."

"I will. Thanks, Sport, see you then."

The rest of the weekend was quiet, and Archer and Jane were definitely getting closer. It had been a long while since Archer felt like this about a woman. He had sworn off love after his girlfriend was killed in retribution for arresting an alleged member of the mob when he worked for the department. It wouldn't be fair to let someone get close. That only made them a target. Granted, he wasn't exactly arresting people these days, but he was still in a dangerous profession, and risking his own life was one thing, but he could no longer allow himself to put someone else in the line of fire. Losing her the way he did almost sent him over the edge. It was a long time before he learned how to deal with that. The Jane factor could be a problem, but at least she was a cop and had received considerable training. Still, he would have to take this slow, no matter what the feeling in his loins had to say about it.

CHAPTER 7

Darla Davis was sitting in the consult room at Dr. Van Landingham's office, and she was growing a little nervous; she had been there too long. The Doctor had taken what seemed like a thousand pictures then suggested a course of action and left the room. Since Mavis set this up, the doctor was sympathetic to her specific needs. She wanted to look different, different enough to fool someone who knew her before. This wasn't going to be as big of a job as she thought. She already looked considerably different than she did 8 years ago, and someone would have to really look close to see she that was the same woman. With a couple of additions and subtractions of a few facial features and some colored contact lenses, no one would be able to tell that Darla Davis was in fact Lydia Crane. The doctor finally returned. He was checking to see that Mavis had the money wired to one of his private accounts. Smiling, he told her that it would only take a day for the procedure, and it would be healed in 3 weeks. She could probably pull it off in 2 if she used makeup properly. He said he could do it tomorrow if she was up to it. She agreed.

By late the next afternoon, she was in her suite with bandages on her face, and she looked like a boxer who should pick another profession. She stayed high on painkillers and booze for the next 2 weeks, only sporadically dancing with her demon; she had Harlan deliver more drugs twice during her recovery time. She remained holed up and hiding out in a narcotic induced haze while Lydia Crane morphed into Darla Davis.

On Monday morning, Archer received a call from Dr. Stephens, who told him that he found traces of Secenol, a powerful sedative, in his system. Archer thanked him for his help and asked him to have his receptionist call Mona with a total, and she would cut him a check and have it sent down to his office today. Then he stopped by The Mug on the drive into his office with Jimmy riding shotgun to find out what he could about the whereabouts of Keri Martin. Once there, Bobbie Mac said he hadn't seen her since the day Doc's daughter was born, which was the previous Thursday. He also said that for four days to go by without her coming in was unusual.

He returned to the office to meet Brody. They were going fishing at Archer's cabin in North Georgia for a week. It was their tradition once a year to go celebrate the anniversary of Archer Security by doing something manly. Last year they went to Wyoming to hunt elk, but this year it was fishing. Archer loved to hunt and fish. It was really a love of the land that had been burned in his soul from when he was a child. He learned how to kill, clean, prepare, and cook deer, boar, and fish when he was twelve years old. His father was an avid hunter who taught him how to track animals and survive in the woods. Archer never killed anything he didn't eat and never killed more than he needed. Sometimes, when several guys went hunting and they ended up with more than they needed, Archer would take it down the road from the cabin and give the meat to a widowed woman who had a bunch of children to feed. In fact, more often than not, Archer would give his deer to her and go home without any for him. He looked forward nowadays to getting back into the woods. Archer had bounced around so much as a kid, sometimes he felt like the woods were his home, because wherever he was during his childhood there were woods, and that's where he spent most of his time growing up.

He was a little bummed about not seeing Jane for a week and considered calling her to come up on the weekend. Brody was in a fight with his Girlfriend DeJour, so Jane would be the only girl up there. She was tough; she could handle that just fine. He had put a couple of agents on his property to watch his house and grounds in case Lydia came back, and Jimmy was going with him, so he was ready to go.

When Archer walked in his office, Brody was waiting in one of the chairs in front of his desk, looking like something out of L.L. Bean. He was wearing a fishing hat with tied flies stuck all over it, and he had on big rubber boots.

"Are you all saddled up and ready to ride?" Brody said with a wide grin.

"Yeah," Archer said while he was looking at Brody's outfit and walked into his private bathroom shaking his head. When he re-emerged, he was dressed in khakis, a linen shirt, and a vest with alot of pockets. He looked about like Brody.

"Let's go."

"I'm way ahead of you, Boss. Trust me; you will be glad I talked you into getting fishing ready now, because with good time we'll be able to fish the little stream by the cabin tonight before dark. And there is a big ole Brookie in there with Brody written all over it"

Within a few minutes they were heading up GA 400 north towards Dahlonega. They exited off one of the last exits on the highway onto a logging road that wrapped around heading up the mountain. The mountains were part of the Blue Ridge Mountains that turned into the Appalachian chain. The native Cherokee Indians called this place Sah-ka-na'-ga, which meant "The Great Blue Hills of God."

About halfway up the mountain, Archer and Brody came around a corner and saw an old woman coming out of the woods. This in itself wouldn't be anything out of the ordinary, as there were hikers all over these mountains; only this woman was at least 80 years old, wearing an old dress and bonnet, and she had a backpack strapped on her. She looked like one of the women from the Old West or some other long ago period in history. After they passed her, Archer looked in the rearview mirror and noticed she had crossed the road and disappeared into the woods on the other side. He remembered thinking how dangerous that must be for a woman her age. They made it on time to fish the little stream, and Archer had to concede that Brody was right about dressing before they came.

Over the next few days, they fished a series of rivers and streams all over the northeast part of the state. They had a very manly week of fishing, getting dirty and peeing outside. On Thursday, Archer decided to call Jane and invite her up for the last couple of days.

"Hello, Lieutenant Yummy. How'd you like to come up to the cabin for the weekend and rough it with me and Brody?" Archer asked.

"Let's see: get away to the beautiful mountains or stay here and look at dead bodies. I think I can come up there and be one of the guys for the weekend."

"Not if I have anything to say about it," he said out of the side of his mouth. "Call Mona, she'll fax you directions."

"OK, I can be there by late tomorrow morning," Jane said.

"Hey, since you're coming up, we're tired of eating fish. Will you stop and pick us up four steaks? If we don't finish them all, Jimmy sure will eat good," he said with a laugh.

"You got it, Handsome. See you soon."

CHAPTER 8

The next day when Jane arrived, Archer was cleaning up after a lunch of fish tacos made from fresh trout. When she pulled up outside the cabin, Jimmy started hopping up and down in front of the door.

"OK, OK, I know, you want to see Jane. I'm coming," Archer said, wiping off his hands on his pants and walking to the door. As soon as he cracked the door, Jimmy shot through the gap and ran to Jane, where he danced in front of her in tight little circles until she reached down and scratched him behind the ear.

"Well, hello, Jimmy. You're such a handsome boy," she said in baby talk.

When she stood up, Jimmy turned and walked proudly back to the house. He smiled when he passed by Archer. Archer rolled his eyes at Jimmy's antics and went to greet Jane.

"Welcome, milady," Archer said in a gallant voice.

"Thank you, kind sir," she replied.

Brody walked out on the front porch and told Archer he had a phone call.

"Did you ever notice the phone rings for you every time I arrive?" Jane pointed out.

"It's just your imagination, now wait here," Archer said, giving her a quick peck before running up the steps and inside.

"Hey, Chief. Jane's got groceries and bags. Help her lug, drag, and carry will you?" Archer said to Brody, then picked the phone up off the counter. Brody went outside and took the bags from Jane.

"Archer," he said into the handset.

"Jon, its Mona, sorry to call you, but one of our employees has a problem that you need to know about. Myra Edwards' grandmother was killed. She lived up at Azalea Park. Myra said that the cook at her diner found her dead in her driveway on Wednesday. He went to check on her when she didn't show up for work for two days. She was beaten with something heavy and died of blunt force trauma to the head."

"Do the police have any leads or suspects?"

"No, that's why I called you; she came to me about it today. She said the police were coming up empty handed. She's scared, Jon, and you should help her. You'll help her, wont you?"

"Of course, Mona, I'm glad you called me. Give her my number here at the cabin and tell her to call right away."

"Will do. She's waiting for my call," Mona said as she hung up the phone.

A few minutes later the phone rang again; it was Myra Edwards.

"Hello, Myra. How you holding up?" Archer said.

Myra Edwards was about 29 years old, had been an employee for 3 years at Archer Security, and had done a good job. She was hired by Archer like all the employees, and was a very intelligent and competent young woman. She was top of her class and majored in criminal justice. She had a problem with the current administration in Washington and wanted to work in the private sector.

"Hi, Mr. Archer. Thank you for speaking with me," Myra said.

"Not at all Myra. Can you tell me anything other than what you told Mona?"

"Yes, I couldn't tell her everything when I was at work today. It's a long story. Do you mind if we meet to talk in person? I don't think I'm very far from you. Mona said you were in the mountains; I live in Azalea Park, and I'm here now," she asked.

"That would be fine. Do you know where

Sahkan'aga Pass is?"

"Yes, about halfway up at the shelf right?"

"That's it. When can you be here?"

"I can be there in about an hour."

He gave her the address and directions.

"Thank you, Mr. Archer," Myra said in an exhausted voice.

"No problem, Myra, and don't worry, we'll find out what happened to your grandmother," Archer said reassuringly.

"I don't know how I can pay you. I know what you charge."

"Don't you worry about a thing. You're part of Archer Security and we take care of our own. Besides, Mona said I had to," he said humbly.

Myra arrived at the cabin a little over an hour later, and Archer met her outside.

"Hello, Myra."

"Hi, Mr. Archer thanks for seeing me."

"Sure, come on in and meet Jane, you already know Brody," Archer said waving her up to the porch. Myra walked inside and Jimmy stood up. Archer stuck out his hand in a stop command to indicate to Jimmy that everything was OK.

"Myra, this is my girlfriend, Jane Kincaid. She's with the Atlanta Police Department," Archer said.

"Hello, nice to meet you. It's good to see you too, Mr. Brody," Myra said.

"You too, Myra. Why don't you have a seat and tell us what's going on, and I'll put on a pot of coffee," Brody said pointing at the chair.

"OK, this is really a fantastic story that was told to me by my Grandmother through a series of conversations that have transpired over the last 15 years. Some she saw and some were told to her by her grandmother. I've never told anyone about any of this, not even my fiancé; it's a huge family secret, so if you don't mind being discreet I would appreciate it. OK, here goes.

"My mother and father died when I was 5, and I went to live with my Grandmother near Dahlonega in Azalea Park. Her name is Henrietta Place Edwards, but she goes by Etta Edwards. She is the granddaughter of Henry Longabough and Etta Place; hence the name Henrietta. In case you don't know who that is; Henry was the Sundance Kid, the partner of Butch Cassidy. I'm sure you've all seen the movie, and Etta was Henry's girlfriend and later his wife. When she returned from South America in 1907, she came back carrying Henry's baby. She went to Denver to a hospital for stomach problems and discovered this. She had the nurse list it as appendicitis for the cause of her visit in case anyone came along asking questions, she was still wanted. Then she moved here to this very mountain and bought a little place, settled in, and had a baby girl named Rosa Place. She named her Rosa after the minister lady in Argentina who performed the ceremony marrying Henry and Etta. The lady wasn't supposed to marry people unless they were Catholic. Henry told her if she did then they would name their firstborn after her, and Etta did just that. She raised Rosa here for seventeen years until Rosa married and had her own baby girl, named Henrietta. Rosa died during childbirth, and the father, not knowing how to care for a baby girl and working long hours everyday panning and digging for gold, asked Etta if the child could live with her. Etta agreed, and Henrietta grew up living with her grandmother, only seeing her father a few times a year, mostly on her birthday and Christmas. That's one of the things we have in common. We were both raised by our grandmothers."

The coffee pot buzzed when it had finished brewing, and Brody got up.

"I'll just be a moment. Cream and sugar, Myra?" he asked.

"Yes, both please."

"Man, you were right this is a fantastic story," Jane said moving in a little closer with wide eyes.

Brody returned with a tray of coffee for everyone and sat down.

"Please continue," Jane said from the edge of her seat.

"Well, as I said, Henrietta's father, William Penn, was a panner. He pan and dug for gold right here on this mountain for over 30 years and was considered by many to be the best there was at finding gold. While others were bringing in dust and pebbles, he was finding nuggets and clumps of the stuff, and somewhere, buried out on the mountain, there's a trunk full of gold nuggets, but I'll get to that in a minute."

Archer and Brody and Jane were just staring at Myra with their mouths hanging open.

"Most people think Butch and Sundance died in South America; they didn't. Sundance died in New York on the day after their return trip to the states in 1915 from poisoning caused by a bullet lodged in his back. Butch finally came to find Etta around 1935 after slinking around out West hiding for twenty years. My grandmother thinks Etta secretly loved Butch as well as Henry. Butch lived with Etta and my grandmother for almost a year. Butch, Sundance, and Etta had come here earlier in life to hideout after a payroll job they pulled at the Castlegate Mining Company. They stayed here for a summer, I believe. After they thought the Pinkertons had given up, and they had gotten bored, they went back out West. They all loved it here so much they wanted to retire here. That was before they had to leave the country and head to South America. The deal was if they ever got split up for any great length of time, and if they didn't know where the others were then they would meet back here to find one another. That's how Butch eventually found Etta.

"Well, Great Grandpa Penn became sick and was dying. He got close to Butch and Etta those last few months before he died. Butch would sit and play cards with him and would bring him whiskey, and Etta would cook for him. Butch would regale him with all of the stories from the old days of Sundance, Etta, and himself and of the rest of the Wild Bunch.

"One night when Butch and Etta went to see him, he was very near death and he told them about the trunk of gold, telling them that he wanted them to have it and to use it if there were any trouble; she agreed. He promised to draw a map for Etta to show her where it was buried.

"A few days later when Butch went to see him for their card game, someone was in his house and Butch could hear him cursing under his breath saying that he knew William had the gold around there somewhere, and he wanted it. Turns out he was William Penn's brother, Walter. He was an alcoholic and a vagrant and caused trouble everywhere he went. William was moved to the hospital and had died the day before and his brother was searching for the gold. Everyone knew William was the best gold man around, and Walter knew that William was a miser and never bought anything he didn't have to, so he figured that gold had to be around there somewhere.

"Butch watched Walter through the window and saw him find the map that William had drawn for Etta. Then Butch followed him up the mountain, keeping out of site. When Walter found the spot where William buried the trunk, Butch waited for him to dig it up. Once he had finished, Butch came out of the brush with his gun drawn and tied Walter's hands behind his back. Then Butch draped him over the horse and tied him down and led him and his horse to the road and slapped the horse on the rump, sending him galloping towards town, bouncing Walter on his back all the way down the road. Butch went back and reburied the gold about 200 yards past the old spot and altered the map. When he came back home, he gave the revised map to Etta and told her what had happened. Butch got bored again and left soon after William died, and Etta never touched the gold or even told anyone about it except for my grandmother,

Henrietta. She told her not to use it unless it was an emergency and then only take what she needed. Henrietta obeyed and didn't use it except for when her husband was dying; she needed some money for his operation. Lately, she's had a lot of doctor bills herself, and since the diner, appropriately named Etta's Place, hasn't been pulling in much money lately, I'm afraid this may have something to do with her death."

"That is a fantastic story, to say the least," Archer said, still trying to absorb what she had just told him. "Myra, I saw a woman Monday afternoon cross the road heading down the mountain wearing and old dress and a bonnet. This lady had on a small backpack like the kind kids carry school books in. Could that have been Etta?"

"Yes, she always wears those old style dresses, and she had a green backpack."

"OK, the cook at Etta's Place, what's his name?" Archer asked, scribbling on a pad with his pen.

"Deuce Williams, he's a nice old man. He's been working for Etta now for twenty years at that diner."

"Do you have the name of the detective working on this case, and has the diner been open since she was killed?"

"Yes, it's been open. There's another lady, Ali, who runs the counter and the register when Etta's not there. And I have the detective's card here somewhere," Myra said rummaging through her purse. She found the card and handed it to Archer.

"OK, why don't you stay for supper? Jane brought steaks, and Brody and I will go to the diner and talk to Deuce Williams. We'll stop by and see the detective on the way. We should be back by supper time. Is that alright with you, Jane?"

"Of course, Handsome. I'll have everything ready when you get back. Are you taking Jimmy with you?"

"No, I'll leave him here to keep an eye on you guys." Jimmy stood up when he heard his name. "You watch out for the girls, OK, buddy?" Archer said, bending down on one knee and scratching Jimmy behind the ear.

"Let's roll, Big Man," Archer said, standing up looking at Brody.

CHAPTER 9

They got in the truck and headed down the mountain. Archer was trying to remember exactly where he saw the woman in the dress. When they got to one particular turn, Archer pulled the truck over and got out. He walked around to the back hatch and opened it. He pulled a piece of old fluorescent orange ribbon out and cut a length about 2 feet long. He walked to the tree line and tied it to a branch. Brody marked the location on the GPS. Then Archer got back in and they headed on down the mountain.

When they reached Azalea Park, they found Etta's Place. They parked in front of the diner.

It was a large room with a counter on one side and a row of booths on the other. The tables had red and white-checkered cloths, and there was a tiny jukebox on every table and several more on the counter. There were pictures from the old west all over the walls, mostly of Butch and Sundance and Etta. There were some pictures of other outlaws and movie stars dressed up in western clothes and there was a huge framed movie poster of Butch Cassidy and the Sundance Kid displayed on the back wall. There was also other western stuff hung everywhere, like saddles and gun belts and bridle straps with a hanging bit.

Archer approached the girl behind the counter, who was writing on an order pad. She was wearing a name tag that read "Ali" and had on a western shirt and skirt with red boots. Cocked on the side of her head was a little straw cowboy hat.

"Hi, Ali. Is Deuce Williams here by any chance?" Archer asked.

She pointed over her shoulder at the big kitchen window with her pen and resumed writing the order.

When Archer and Brody walked through the swinging kitchen doors, they saw an old man in his late 60s with gray hair and gray whiskers standing at the grill tending to some burgers.

"Excuse me, sir, are you Deuce Williams?" Archer asked.

"Depends on who's asking," he replied, looking Archer up and down.

"I'm Jon Archer, and this is my partner Brody. We are with Archer Security."

"Oh, yes, yes, from that big security firm in Atlanta, the one that Myra runs, right?" he said with a wide smile as he grabbed Archer's hand and started pumping it vigorously.

Archer and Brody looked at each other.

'Um, yes, that's it. Say, Deuce, Myra asked us

to try and find out what happened to Etta," Archer stated.

"Yeah, poor ole thing. Miss Etta sure was a sweet lady."

"Myra said you last saw her on Monday, is that right?"

"It sure is. She left work early on Monday and that's the last time I saw her alive, God rest her soul."

"Did she say where she was going when she left early?"

"No, she was talking on the phone to the hospital; she told them she would be by to pay her bill this week. Then she made another call, but I don't know who it was to."

"Was anyone else here when she left?"

"Yeah, a couple of guys were at the counter. Let's see... there was Mr. Caruthers – he owns the muffler shop across the street – and that quiet fellow Harold."

"What quiet fellow? Who do you mean?" Archer asked.

"That quiet fellow that moved here about a year ago with his wife. His name is Harold, never seen her. He's been in every morning since he got here; he always wears a Nebraska Cornhuskers hat. Come to think of it, I haven't seen him since that Monday." They walked back out through the swinging doors again

"Where was he sitting at the counter?"

"Right here in this first seat."

"And where was the phone that Miss Etta used to make the calls from?"

"Right here," he answered, pointing just inside the swinging doors. The phone and the stool he pointed out were hardly four feet from each other.

"Would you happen to know where Harold lives, Deuce?"

"Somewhere out on the lake, I heard the mailman say one day when someone mentioned how quiet and secretive he is. He said that Harold had a brand new house built and a new dock. He drives an old El Camino, red. Take the first right when you head out of town, and it will take you all the way around the lake. You'll find it," Deuce said with confidence.

"One other thing, I just remembered it: when I came back in from changing the specials on the marquis outside, Harold was standing behind the counter by the door. I asked what he was doing; he said he was looking for a Styrofoam cup for his coffee. I think he was eavesdropping on Miss Etta's call," Deuce said with a suspicious look in his eye.

"Thanks, Deuce. You've been a big help," Archer said and shook his hand.

"What is that wonderful smell?" Brody asked looking towards the oven.

"That's peach cobbler." Deuce said with a big smile. "Best in the state, let me box up a piece to take with you."

"Sir, you are saint."

Archer rolled his eyes and walked out.

They drove down to the Azalea Park Police Station and parked on the side of the building. They walked in, and Archer presented the card that Myra had given him to the Desk Sergeant, while Brody stood behind him wiping peach cobbler crumbs off his shirt.

"Have a seat and he'll be out when he can," the Desk Sergeant said in a cavalier voice.

"Tell him we may have information on the murder of Etta Edwards," Archer said and winked at Brody.

The Sergeant picked up the phone and spoke softly for a few seconds and hung up. Detective Sommers came out of a door marked "Officers only" and looked at the Desk Sergeant, who pointed at Archer.

Detective Sommers was about 35 years old, but he looked 15. He weighed about 125 lbs and was somewhere around 5"5' with a pencil thin moustache and beady little black dots for eyes. He stood with his hands on his hips and acted like he was ten feet tall.

"Hello, gentlemen. I'm Detective Sommers."

"I'm Jon Archer, this is my partner Brody. We're with Archer Security in Atlanta. We are investigating the murder of Etta Edwards. I wanted to introduce myself and inform you of our intentions. We find the local law enforcement usually appreciates it when we announce ourselves."

A nervous look washed over his face.

"I've heard of you guys. I've seen you on the news in that case with the attorney and that mafia guy. I probably don't need to tell you, but I will anyway, this is still an ongoing investigation, and we don't need any outside interference. I'm sure you understand. The Desk Sergeant said you may have some information for me."

"Nothing concrete yet, just a theory."

"Would you like to share?" asked Sommers.

"Not until I can confirm my suspicions. I wouldn't want to interfere. I'm sure you understand," Archer said with a smile, and he and Brody walked out. They got in the truck and pulled around the building across the street and came up through the alley to where they could see the front door to the police station. They were hidden behind some multi - colored streamers that were tied to the guy wire in preparation of the upcoming Founder's Day Parade.

"What are you doing? You're up to something sneaky."

"Smart money says Boy Wonder in there will be coming out any minute and lead us right to Harold," Archer said.

"What makes you think that?"

"A couple of reasons, dear Watson. One, he didn't ask who hired us; two, all he did was ask us what we know and tell us to stay away, and three, he was wearing a University Of Nebraska ring. I'm not only betting he knows Harold, I'm betting he's related to him."

A few minutes later, Sommers came out of the station and looked up and down the street before getting in his cruiser and making a u-turn and heading out of town.

Brody just shook his head and said with a laugh, "That's why you make the big bucks, Boss."

They followed the cruiser halfway around the lake from behind a truck so as not to be seen, until it reached a house with a mailbox that read Sommers. Archer pulled into a park across the street behind a pavilion. The Officer got out and walked toward the house. Just then, a U-Haul truck pulled in the driveway, and a man got out and went inside; Brody was taking snapshots with a digital camera with a telephoto lens. Archer looked at Brody and smiled.

"They're going to run," Archer said.

"That could be the detective's house. You don't know that it's Harold's place."

Just then Sommers and another guy came out talking to each other rather heatedly. Sommers was using his hands and pointing while giving the other fellow the what-for. The other guy just stood there with his hands in his pockets and his head down, quietly listening in his dirty Nebraska Cornhuskers hat. It was a strange site seeing such a little man giving a rash of shit to such a huge man who just stood there sheepishly and looked like a little boy in trouble for breaking a window.

"Call your girl at the phone company and get a list of the phone calls made from Etta's Place from Monday on," Archer said to Brody.

Brody got on his phone and a few minutes later he was looking at a small list of numbers on his laptop and started calling them. The first one was Myra's voicemail, then the regional hospital, and the third one was Zack's Gold and Pawn Shop. Bingo!

"Now do the same thing for this address for Monday, Tuesday, and Wednesday," he said, pointing at the Sommer's mailbox. Brody obliged and the list only had two numbers on it, one Archer recognized from the business card for the detective that Myra had given him. The other was Zack's Gold and Pawn called on Tuesday morning.

"He's had plenty of time to get rid of the gold. It's been five days. Let's go," Archer said, cranking up the truck.

They backed up, turned around, and headed for the highway leading out of town, stopping when they reached Zack's.

They went in the front door. It was a typical pawnshop. The room was large with a showcase of knives and guns stretching along the whole back wall. There were rows and rows of short shelving units running the length of the room. They were stacked with everything: radios, TV sets, CD and DVD players, and every kind of power tool you could imagine. There were Georgia Bulldog pictures and posters pinned on almost all of the available real estate on the walls. They stepped up to the counter, and Archer asked the man behind the counter if he was Zack.

Zack was in his early sixties and proud to be southern. He had worn out jeans and cowboy boots that were so old they had flattened out to the point where the stitching had frayed. He wore a black University of Georgia ball cap and had a chaw of Red Man in his cheek. He wore a flannel shirt and a black windbreaker with yellow letters reading CAT on the breast, and it looked like he wore it all summer long. He turned down the radio that was whining out an old Buck Owens song.

"Who's asking?' he said from behind the counter.

Archer just rolled his eyes like he was getting tired of that answer and shook his head. "Look, receiving stolen property is so far the only charge you're facing, but it could get alot worse."

"Whoa, whoa, whoa. I don't even know who you are or what you're talking about. I get a photo-copy of a driver's license on every item I take in, just like I'm supposed to."

"Good, Zack. Then you won't mind showing me a receipt and the photocopy of a license from the guy who sold you some gold in the last couple days."

"Yesterday. He called the other day and I told him it would take a couple days to get the cash. It was twenty five thousand dollars. Yep, I can not only show you the receipt, but I can show you the gold. I called the police while the guy was here from the back room because it was the same type stuff that Miss Etta had brought in before, and she called me about some gold she wanted to bring in on the day she died. I can't be sure but I think it's in her backpack. I had heard she was killed so when he showed it to me, I called it in. The Detective said that he knew of some gold she had sold to a guy, and it was alright to buy it from him. That's all I knew until he called back just a few minutes ago and said he wanted to come by here and see it," he said and he put the file back in the drawer that he had shown Archer.

"He's coming here today?"

"Yeah, he's on his way now. You can ask him about it when he gets here. Look, I'm a good guy. I play by the rules, and I don't tolerate no monkey business. That's why I called the police."

Archer whispered something to Brody and Brody walked quickly outside.

"OK, Zack, I'm sorry. I switched to Decaf today and I'm a little edgy. I'm trying to find out what happened to Etta. Her granddaughter works for me and she asked me to help her get to the bottom of all this. Now, how well do you know this detective?" Archer asked.

"Hardly at all. He's only been here a couple years, and he transferred in from somewhere out in the Midwest."

"Zack, I believe this man may want to cause you harm when he gets here. Either to kill you and take you're gold, or frame you for Etta's murder. I think it was his brother Harold that killed Miss Etta and stole her gold, then sold it to you. The detective knows we're closing in on him and his brother. Do you have any Kevlar?"

"You bet your ass I do, and I'm always armed when I'm here."

"Good. Wear it and don't do anything unless he tries something first. I'm just saying be ready. So far we have nothing on him that's not circumstantial. Can I see the backpack?"

"Yeah, come on. I never did like that little piss ant anyway," he said as he was rounding the counter and gathering up a vest that was hanging from a hook in the back of the door to the office. He put the vest on and a jacket on over that. They went into the office to a huge safe, and, after a minute of twisting the dial, he swung the door open and Archer stopped him and put on some latex gloves before touching the backpack. Upon inspection, Archer saw that the backpack had specks and smudges of blood on it, and it was the same one he saw the woman crossing the road wearing.

"Make sure your security cameras are on, and if you have a way to record audio, do it. If he tries to arrest you, tell him you request another officer be present. Also, if you have a handcuff key, it wouldn't hurt to hide it on your person."

Zack was staring at him with his eyes wide open, nodding.

"Wrap this in plastic without touching it and put it back in the safe," Archer said, handing the backpack to Zack by the glove.

"The Cavalry is on their way," Brody said, walking back inside.

"OK. The State Police are on their way here now. I'm going to stay out of sight when Sommers gets here. Brody, you go keep an eye on our friend out by the lake until the boys get here. That U-Haul truck wasn't for unloading, and when he leaves I'll bet he's not coming back. This is happening now. Maybe we can bag these two and be back to the cabin by supper-time," Archer said.

"Right, Boss. I'm on it," Brody replied as he left again. He jumped in the truck and drove off toward the lake. When he was halfway through town, he passed the detective going the other way. They both slowed and glared at each other as they passed. Each one looked at the other like they had business with him, but didn't have time to deal with it right now.

Brody rolled out to Harold's place on the lake and resumed his position beside the pavilion in the park. He backed up into the shadows under a magnolia tree and pulled out the binoculars. There were some prisoners carrying boxes and furniture out of the house and into the U-Haul truck parked in Harold's driveway. Harold was bugging out quick with the help of the county. He was hurrying in and out of the house yelling at the convicts and cursing loudly. After the truck was full, he loaded up the prisoners in the back of his pickup and drove around to the other side of the lake to a prison bus that was parked for a county work detail. Harold got out of the truck and was talking to a hack that was holding a shotgun and sitting up on a horse. The hack bent down and Harold handed him something.

Brody got out of Archer's truck and decided to take a look inside Harold's house while he was across the lake. He moved quickly across the street and down by the basement door on the side of the house. He checked the door, but it was locked, so he jimmied the knob lock and then picked the deadbolt, disappearing inside. Once inside, he saw a long narrow hallway stretching the back length of the house. There were several doors on either side, each with a small security window in the middle of the top quadrant of the doors; it looked like a lockdown unit at a mental hospital. Brody stood on his toes and peered in the window of the first door. Inside the dark room he saw something move against the back wall in the shadows. He couldn't tell what it was, but he knew one thing for sure: it had eyes.

CHAPTER 10

Archer was waiting outside the pawnshop by a window behind an old freezer unit when the detective pulled up. Sommers got out of the cruiser and entered the shop.

"Hello, Detective. I guess you're here to see that gold I called you about," Zack said smiling.

"Yes, and I want to see the paperwork from this transaction, too," Sommers ordered.

"Alrighty, here you go," he said, handing him the file with the receipt and photocopies from the drawer.

"Thank you. Zack, is it?" he asked and it was clear that he could care less.

"Yes, sir, owner and operator."

"Zack, do you have any security video from

yesterday from when the guy was here?"

"Of course I do," Zack answered.

Archer cringed when he heard Zack's answer.

"Good, good. Then why don't you get me that tape and today's tape, too, if you don't mind."

"Today's tape? Why do you want that?" Zack asked with a confused look on his face.

Sommers pulled his gun from its holster. Zack lost the confused look from his face, and his eyes grew wide. He swallowed hard and said "They're in the office," as he started moving toward the door that had sticker letters reading: No Admittance.

"I'll be right behind you, so don't get cute."

"Why are you doing this?" Zack said acting dumb and playing it pretty well.

"It's a shame you had to resort to a life of crime, Zack. That's what they'll say after I shoot you and put one of your guns in your hand. Once I destroy the evidence of the sale, then I will be able to name you as the one who killed that old woman and tried to shoot me when I confronted you about it, leaving me with no choice but to kill you. Now, let's have those tapes, and then I'll take the gold. See, unfortunately, when I take that gold into evidence, there will only be about half as much in there as there is now," he said with a loud laugh.

Archer saw them disappear into the office through the window, and then a State Police car pulled up to the curb. There were two more behind it. Archer ran over and spoke with the deputy. He instructed the other deputies to go around to the rear entrance and cover the back, and he and Archer went through the front door of Zack's Gold and Pawn.

Brody turned on his flashlight and pointed it through the tiny window of the first door. He couldn't believe what he was seeing: there were four children of various ages all chained together with leg shackles. Their hair was long and stringy, and they had grown out of their shabby clothes long ago; the older ones were missing teeth. They were filthy and very malnourished. Their sunken, hollow little faces shrank from the light, and their eyes had the look of an animal. Brody tried the knob, but it was locked. It was a metal security door, and there was no way he could break it down. He was going to try to signal to the children inside to wait and that he would be back, but they weren't even aware of his presence.

He moved further down the hall, pointing the light in the windows. In the room across from the children was a woman who must've been in her forties. From the look in her eyes, her condition was worse than the children's. Physically, she looked the same, but the look in her eye was one of pure terror; someone had inflicted traumatic harm on her at a level usually reserved for prisoners of war and medieval torture chamber victims. He checked the lock and moved on to the next door and looked inside. There was a young woman in her late twenties, unconscious. She was at least 8 months pregnant. Her face was scarred from repeated beatings, and her lips were swollen to twice their normal size. There was a big, round, dried blood stain on the front of her dress, and she laid on the floor in a big puddle of urine. Brody looked down at his watch and realized he had been in there for too long, and he quickly looked in the last window. There was an older man in a state trooper's uniform. His clothes were covered in blood, and his face was completely bruised up. The man in the uniform looked up at Brody's eyes and pleaded for help. Brody couldn't hear what the man was saying, but he knew what he wanted. Brody nodded and went back to the door leading outside. He eased it open and looked through the crack. He saw Harold's pickup pulling up in the driveway. He pulled out his cell phone. No service signal. He heard the door to the house slam shut above him. There was nowhere to hide and the footsteps that were growing louder stopped in front of the door at the top of the stairs.

Archer and the deputy from the State Police stopped outside of the office long enough to hear Sommers tell Zack he would see him in hell. They burst through the door guns drawn and got the drop on Sommers. He was standing with the backpack of gold in one hand and the other was holding the gun pointed at Zack. When he saw Archer draw down on him, without missing a beat Detective Sommers put the barrel of his service revolver in his mouth and pulled the trigger. Parts of his head and a spray cloud of blood slathered the safe behind him, and his body fell to the floor, landing with his eyes wide open, still looking at Archer. After Archer gave the full story to the deputies, he tried again to reach Brody, but was unsuccessful.

"Say Deputy, the other perp is at home trying to bug out. I have a man on him, and we need to get there pretty quick. But I haven't heard from my man in a while and can't reach him on the cell. Do you mind if we ride out there together?"

"We were waiting for a warrant. We just got it. Lots of back up and Internal Affairs are coming, and they're almost here, and they'll want to have a long conversation with you, so we better go now. You're welcome to ride with me."

"Thanks, I will," Archer replied, and he tried Brody again.

Brody decided to try and get the jump on Harold when he opened the door to the staircase, so he climbed to the top of the stairs. When Harold swung the door slowly open, he saw Brody's shadow on the wall move when Brody raised his gun and slammed it shut again. Brody decided not to take any more chances with this psycho and shot a round through the door that Harold was stupid enough to still be standing behind. Wood splintered in Harold's face, and the round sank high into his chest right below his collarbone. Harold rolled around out of the way and ran to the pantry holding one arm up with the other. He grabbed a double barrel twelve gauge that had seen a hacksaw and checked the breech; it was loaded. He went back to the staircase, listening for noise. He had the shotgun pointed at the door when Brody's cell phone rang on the other side. Brody bent down to try and stop the noise when the first shot blew a huge hole in the door, going right over his head.

"Did you meet the family?" Harold screamed in a crazy voice.

"Oh, yeah. You should be proud. Say, does being a big Pussy run in your family – or did you slowly turn that way? I mean, any man who locks up women, children, and old people has got to be a yellow bellied Pussy, right?" Brody said, then started to back down, one step at a time so he didn't make any noise.

"What's your big plan, Dickhead?" Harold yelled through the hole in the door.

"Well, Son, if you put down that sweeper, I'm gonna tear your eyes out and shove 'em up your tookus so you get a real good view of me kicking your ass. Then I'm going to have you arrested and make sure they take 'Old Sparky" out of retirement and light you up until you bleed brains out of your eyes and shit yourself. Then we will try to bring these people back to some kind of sane reality they can call a life. Or, I'll just fucking shoot you myself...I haven't decided yet"

Then the second blast came splintering through the door and grazed the top of Brody's shoulder, sending him toppling down the stairs. When he came to rest at the foot of the stairs, his back was against the wall and he was facing Harold, who was peering through the hole in the door like one of those picture boards at the fair that you stick your face into to have your photograph taken. Brody raised his gun and fired one single shot, hitting Harold in the teeth and severing his spinal cord. Harold fell forward and took the door off of the hinges, riding it down the stairs toward Brody. Brody rolled out of the way and fired three more shots into Harold. Brody heard car doors slamming and people rushing in, and Archer appeared at the top of the stairs holding his gun up.

"Where are you, Sport?!!" Archer yelled.

"I'm down here. I'm hit. It's not bad; I've cut

myself shaving worse than this. We're still going to need a few ambulances though, enough to carry seven or eight. We also need family services here. You ain't gonna believe this shit down here. Did the dirty detective show up?"

"We caught him red handed trying to pin the whole thing on Zack and kill him. Instead of going down, that chicken shit ate the barrel of his service revolver. What do you mean enough for seven or eight? " Archer said as he and the deputy helped Brody to his feet.

Brody felt around on Harold's person and found a retractable ring of keys attached to his belt. He snapped the cable line and started down the hall.

"Come on. We need to get these people out now. This sick rat fuck has apparently kept these people chained up for God knows how long. One is a state trooper for God's sake. Four of them are children; I mean, this whole thing is fubar and this guy is a certified wing nut, Boss."

They helped everyone out of the locked rooms and up the stairs where the ambulances were pulling up. The woman was his wife, who had been on lockdown for 15 years. She had two kids while in that condition. Needless to say she was a strong woman. The younger woman was a hitchhiker he picked up in Lincoln almost two years ago. The patrolman tried to ask him too many questions at a truck stop driving from Nebraska to Georgia a year ago. And the four malnourished children were Harold's. Turns out the youngest child was born from the hitchhiker. He kept them locked up 24 hours a day. He left them each with a pail to use as a bathroom that he would empty about every week and he would return it rinsed out with some scraps of food in it, except for the children. They had to all share two pails. He washed their clothes while they waited naked once a month. This was their existence.

Harold had to leave Nebraska in a hurry; some neighbors were getting too nosy. The old house wasn't anywhere near as secure as this one, and he didn't feel safe there anymore. He blackmailed his brother, the detective, into letting him come to Georgia and helping him with his dirty little secret by threatening to tell the cops at the station why he really had to transfer from Nebraska. It seems that the detective took a fancy to small children. They didn't have enough to indict him, but they suggested he turn in his resignation. Harold told the builder that the basement in his new home was for dorm rooms to rent out to students at the college to earn extra money. Harold's sick reign of terror was over for those seven people; Brody saw to that. But the consolation prize of life isn't worth much when your spirit is broken and every noise sends you into a nervous breakdown, striking you rigid with fear.

Archer promised the state police they would come down in a couple days to the state courthouse and give a full statement. The bad guys were dead, and it was the weekend, so the paperwork would have to wait until Monday.

Archer and Brody made it back to the cabin for supper. Jane told them that they had just put the steaks on. The girls had had a lazy afternoon sitting on the porch and having a glass of wine talking about everything under the sun.

"Did you find anything out about Etta?" Jane asked.

Archer and Brody looked at each other and shook their heads.

"Yes, we did, but I need a shower and Brody needs a little medical attention. After that, we can sit down to eat and we'll tell you both the whole story," Archer said, walking up the stairs. Jane tended to Brody's shoulder and set the table for supper.

Archer told the entire story over dinner, and, as they were finishing dessert, he continued.

"So, the detective got spooked when we let him know we were on the case, too, and he tried to set up the pawnshop owner to take the rap for your grandmother's murder and then he was going to kill him. Then he was going to turn in only half of the gold. By destroying the receipts and tapes, no one would have any way to know how much gold there should be, and with Zack dead the detective and his brother would have the twenty five grand and half of the gold scot free – and those poor people would still be held captive."

"Ah, but they aren't because you and Brody showed up in the nick of time to save the day," Jane added.

"I still can't believe you wrapped it all up in one day," Myra said.

"That's because once they knew we were involved they realized they were no longer in control, and they got scared and started making stupid mistakes," Brody concluded.

"Well, thank you, Mr. Archer and Mr. Brody,

for all of your help."

"No problem, Myra. Glad we could help. I'm going to send Doc back up in the morning to find the gold. We marked the trail to it on the road and the GPS. I'll have him take it to a broker I know and get you market value and have a check deposited in a savings account at the same bank where we do the automatic deposit for your paycheck. Will that be alright?" Archer asked.

"That would be fine, and thank you. I'll ask Doc to save out a couple pieces of gold for you that I insist you take as payment. At least you can say you have a chunk of gold that was owned by Butch Cassidy and Etta Place."

"OK, that is cool. Deal. Thank you, Myra."

Brody started to pout.

"You too, Mr. Brody. That's why I said a couple pieces."

Brody's pout melted into a smile.

CHAPTER 11

Darla put on a black dress she bought in a boutique in the hotel lobby, some high heels, and the contact lenses she had ordered. She was ready to meet Thomas Reynolds. She walked down through the lobby of the Marriott and across the street to Gibney's, catching the eyes of more than a few men. It was 4:45.

There were two entrances to Gibney's, one from the mall upstairs on the inside and one from the street level. Knowing Reynolds would be coming down from the Athletic Club upstairs, Darla placed herself at the bar on the far end. Reynolds would have to pass right by her from where she was seated; there was a mirror on the back wall of the bar with rows and rows of liquor bottles lined up in front of it. From her vantage point she could see over the bottles and would see him coming a full fifteen steps before brushing by her. She made small talk with Eddie, the owner, who was a little irritated that his bartender was late, forcing him to cover behind the bar. He was polite and asked the usual questions: Are you from here? Are you staying across the street? What brings you to town? She leaked a little bit of information at a time. She was from New Jersey. Here in town to consider some business ventures. Retired for the last five years. She kept noticing herself in the mirror, and it was so strange to her to see Darla staring back at Lydia.

A few of the slightly drunk and extremely brave approached her with obnoxious compliments and terrible pick up lines. They were systematically gunned down one at a time and it didn't take long for everyone to know that she wasn't there to play. She drank one White Russian in a hurry, and in front of her she had a second that she was sipping very slowly. When she saw him coming down the stairs, she avoided looking at the mirror for more than a second or two at a time as he approached, in case he was watching her; he was. She waited for just the right moment and casually slipped off her barstool; as soon as he was right behind her, she turned and stepped out in the aisle. Luckily, his head was half turned around, talking to a squirrelly-looking guy behind him in a suit with horned rimmed glasses; he was clearly a lackey. As she stepped out, she raised her glass chest level, and when he collided into her, the White Russian completely covered the front of her black dress. She gasped and inhaled as if it were made of liquid nitrogen.

By the time he realized what had happened, Darla reached on the bar, grabbing a glass of something yellow, and threw it in the face of Thomas Reynolds.

"It's customary, sir, to apologize to a lady after you've accosted her. I thought you men had manners in the South," screeched Darla as she was tearing up.

Then, before he could speak, she ran out of the side entrance. She would let him chew on that for a few days and then take another swing at him.

At the bar, Thomas called Eddie over to his end, opposite from where Darla was sitting.

"Who was that?" asked Thomas

"Don't know her name. She's been here for a little while. She's from out of town, and she's some kind of businesswoman. Retired, that's all I know. Couple of guys tried to run her up, but she wasn't having it," answered Eddie. "She's a classy one, that's for sure."

"She is striking, isn't she?" Thomas said.

"You know it, Mr. Reynolds."

"Eddie please don't call me that. It's Thomas. How long have we known each other anyway? You're a friend of mine, for God's sake."

"When I'm back here, behind the bar, it's Mr. Reynolds," Eddie said humbly as he put a martini in front of him.

"You're a man of honor, Eddie," Thomas declared as he raised his glass. "Eddie, when the lady comes back, please ask her if she would allow me to apologize, buy her a new drink, and pay for the dry cleaning of her dress. I wouldn't want to do anything to damage or sully the reputation and good standing of southern gentlemen. Here's my card to give her."

"Of course."

The following Monday, Darla walked into Gibney's at 7 PM. When she saw Thomas at the end of the bar, she turned around and walked back out. He saw this and followed her out.

"Ma'am, please wait. I must apologize for the other evening," Thomas said with sincerity.

Darla stopped and waited at the curb with her arms folded and one raised eyebrow.

"I guess a man in my position is a little skeptical of women in bars, but that's my problem. I am truly sorry for not apologizing right away."

"Look, I don't care who you are or what the hell kind of position you're in. I won't tolerate rudeness. Now, that being said, I guess I was a little hard on you," Darla said.

"Not at all. It was my clumsiness, and I should be flogged for not noticing such a beautiful woman in the first place," Thomas said smoothly.

"See? Just like that the dignity of the South has been preserved."

"Please allow me to at least buy you another drink."

"I can buy my own drink, thank you. But if it's a truce you're suggesting, I'll order us both one, and we can toast the salvation of the South," she said with a little smile.

Two hours later they were still engrossed in conversation, flirting back and forth.

"So, why is a beautiful, smart Princeton grad starting a new life in Atlanta?" Thomas said with a warm smile.

She exhaled heavily and managed to squeeze out a tear. "My husband and I had a financial consulting firm together in the World Trade Center. On 9/11, I was out of the country meeting with clients in Japan. My husband and eleven of our employees were killed. It shattered me, and I have been retired for the past five years trying to reinvent myself and move on."

"Oh, my God. I'm so sorry. I had no idea," Thomas said sympathetically.

"No, no, it's OK. You couldn't have known."

"Please, please don't take this the wrong way, but…I'm glad you came here."

"Well, I know what you mean. And I have to say, I'm glad I met you, too."

"Pardon my forwardness, Darla, but I find you completely refreshing. Would you have dinner with me?"

"I'd love to," she replied.

He made a call on his cell phone, and a few minutes later a limousine pulled up out front. She asked Eddie for her tab, and Thomas shook his head behind her.

"You're a friend of Thomas's now, so your money's no good here anymore," said Eddie.

"Well, thank you very much Eddie. But I insist on leaving a tip for the most gracious service," she said as she threw a twenty down and winked at him and they turned to leave.

They talked more than they ate at the restaurant – about everything – and it wasn't too difficult for Lydia to keep turning the subject of the conversation back to him. The next thing they knew, they were the only ones in the place except for a couple of waiters and a manager that wanted to go home. They didn't dare approach Mr. Reynolds's table and try and hurry them. They just kept refilling their coffee and smiling. At the end of the night, between passionate kisses, she agreed to come out to his house on the weekend.

The only thing left to do was set the hook.

The next couple of weeks were filled with dinners, parties, and a weekend getaway, and they all seemed to blur together for Darla and Thomas. Thomas was genuinely happy. He had never met a woman who was so indifferent as to whether he liked her or not. So much so that he called Dan and Peter Westbrook, his business partners, in his office for a meeting. Dan and Peter were twin brothers, and Thomas had known them since college.

"Gentlemen, as you know I have been seeing quite a bit of Darla Davis. Also, I'm turning 65 years old weekend after next. I thought when Gretchen died I would never marry again, but in light of the new found feelings I have for Darla, I've decided to fly to Las Vegas this weekend and marry that woman. Peter, I know you've been having some medical problems, and you shouldn't really be traveling, at least until you see that specialist in Chicago. So, I'm going to ask you, Dan, to be my best man. The following weekend we will have a party at my house to celebrate the marriage and my birthday. There, I would like you Peter, to give a toast."

'It will be an honor, you old rascal," replied Dan.

"Likewise," Peter said.

"Good, it's all set then," Thomas beamed.

Later that afternoon the phone rang at Archer Security.

"Good afternoon, Archer Security," Mona said cheerfully.

"Hi, Mona, this is Dan Westbrook. Is Archer in?"

After a moment, Archer was on the phone

"Archer."

"Hello, Archer. Dan Westbrook here. I was wondering if you could do me a favor and keep it outside the company business?"

'What have you got in mind?" asked Archer.

"I want you to find out what you can on a woman named Darla Davis." Dan went on to explain.

"Dan, are you sure you guys don't need some body men?"

"No, no just check her out."

Archer made some notes and received a fax from Dan. He called Doc into his office and filled him in on what Dan said. Doc had been working on a case involving a high profile attorney who was receiving death threats from the associates of an alleged member of the mob, who he couldn't get off on a murder rap. No one could have gotten him off. He was caught by the police standing over the body holding the murder weapon yelling at the corpse. Two cops testified on the stand that he said, "If you weren't dead, I would kill you again." His associates were convinced he was working both sides, and a competent lawyer could have gotten an acquittal. Doc had been his body man for the last month and thwarted two different attempts on the man's life. One attempt landed Doc in the hospital from a gunshot wound. He was wearing his Kevlar but a round hit him in the shoulder. Doc was quietly happy about being pulled off the protection detail and given some good old fashion detective work to do. It was alot safer, and digging for information and getting people to talk were Doc's specialties. He left Archer's office and started turning over the life of Darla Davis.

CHAPTER 12

Thomas Reynolds had stopped by his office to pick up some documents he would need for a marriage certificate and to pick up Dan to go to the airport. Darla was waiting in the common area of Reynolds Enterprises, standing at the coffee station right across the hall from Dan Westbrook's office.

"I'm not saying there's anything wrong with her. I'm just concerned for Thomas. Peter, you know as well as I do that he wears his heart on his sleeve, and he loses all common sense when it comes to women he's in love with. Which happens to be anyone who stands up to him. I just don't want to see him get hurt. That's why I'm checking up on her," Dan said.

Darla's ears pricked up.

"I've got our security firm working on this, but I haven't heard back from Jon Archer yet."

Dan concluded by saying, "I'll let you know what I find out, OK? Goodbye, Peter."

Darla was furious; he had to be talking about her, no question about it. She went to Thomas's office and said she would wait for him downstairs at the car. As soon as she got in the elevator, she pulled out her cell phone and dialed. As she walked through the lobby she was getting judgmental looks and hearing whispers from the employees, then an uninterested sounding voice answered the phone.

"Hello?"

"This is Darla; I need to speak to Mavis."

"Keep the phone near you. She'll call you in a few minutes," the voice said.

Darla hung up the phone; she was a little more than worried. This was trouble for sure, and Archer of all people. What were the odds on that?

By the time she reached the limo, the phone rang. It was Mavis. She circled around behind the car instead of getting in.

"What's the problem?" asked Mavis.

"Could be big trouble. I overheard Dan West-brook, Thomas's partner, talking on the phone to his brother, his other partner; he's onto me."

"How much does he know?" asked Mavis.

"Only that there's something he doesn't trust

about me. Get this: he has his security firm running a check on me. The worst part is its Jon Archer's security firm!" exclaimed Lydia.

"Ha, ha, ha. Holy Shit! That's great," Mavis said with a loud laugh.

"How's that great?"

"Because he'll be around asking you questions, and he won't even recognize you – and when I get out in a little while, we are seriously going to fuck him up."

"Ohhh, I have waited so long for that. I might have to do to him what I did to old Lester," said Lydia.

"You'll be smarter this time."

"What about for now?"

"We've covered that. If they check, they'll find what we wanted them to find."

"Yeah, if they only check the last fifteen or twenty years, but what if they dig real deep? Darla Davis doesn't exactly have a first grade report card, you know," said Lydia.

"If they ask, say that before high school you were living abroad on an American Army Base; that'll explain having no accent. I'll have the hacker input a file on…let's say William Grant Davis, a Sergeant stationed in Germany during those years. Since Archer was military, they will check that for sure, and it'll check out."

"OK, that might work for the security team. What about Dan Westbrook? He's a nosy little prick."

"We may have to add him to the list; here's what I want you to do."

Lydia listened intently.

"OK, I can't wait to see you. Bye."

Darla ended the call and speed dialed her phone again, "Do you know who this is?"

"Sure, you're the only number programmed in this phone. You're Rooster's broad, right?" said Mac. Mac was a machine, it was all in a day's work for him. It wasn't anything personal; it was a job. He was a problem solver. At 6'3", 280 lbs, he was mostly muscle and not too well educated, but he was smart, which served him well at his job. He went through a job burning all jets on high. He was an Italian American who was short on patience and thrived financially and personally on administering retribution for someone else, as long as the check cleared.

"That's right. Listen, we have to take care of Dan Westbrook now. He's become a liability."

"I understand. I'll take care of it. His info is in the file."

"We are leaving town now to go to Las Vegas. Dan is coming back late Saturday evening," said Darla.

"Consider it done. One more question: do you

want it to be nice, or do you want it to be nasty?" Mac said coolly.

"If it's not nasty, it's not done right," she answered without a hint of mercy.

"Nasty it is."

"Thanks. I'll be in touch," and she hung up as if she had just ordered a pizza.

Thomas walked out of the building followed by a smiling Dan Westbrook and they rode out to Peachtree DeKalb Airport and boarded the company jet headed for Las Vegas. All the way there, Dan sat at the opposite end of the cabin from Darla and Thomas and whispered into a satellite phone. She would catch him looking directly at her while he was talking, and offer up a fake smile when she looked back at him.

Yeah, you just keep smiling, you meddlesome motherfucker. You're about to become recently deceased.

Later that night, Thomas and Darla gathered with the rest of their party and were married at the Bellagio Hotel. With Thomas's family and friends as witnesses, Darla had no one representing her, and she had to use the wedding coordinator as a maid of honor. Everyone was glad-handing Thomas and kissing his ass, which was the norm everywhere they went. Darla couldn't wait to get back home. The next afternoon, Dan headed back for home while the newlyweds stayed on for a few days to relax. They were to have a proper honeymoon in a few weeks after Thomas's birthday, but Thomas told Dan they wanted a couple of days alone before going back to Atlanta. Darla just wanted to make it through the weekend without vomiting.

CHAPTER 13

Mac drove slowly through the North Druid Hills neighborhood in the Hummer he had stolen from a parking structure on Lavista road. He had left his car in a nearby lot. He drove to Dan's house and circled back to what he calculated would be a ten-minute walk from where he was going and wrote the address of a large, empty looking house on a corner. He then drove back to Dan's place and waited across the street.

About an hour and a half later, Dan came pulling up in the driveway in his Mercedes. As Dan idled and waited for the garage door to open, he saw the lights from the Hummer racing up behind him and the deafening sound of metal twisting confused him at first and seemed to happen in slow motion. The Hummer was spinning his wheels and throwing alot of smoke in the air as it rammed the Mercedes into the inside wall of Dan's garage. By the time Dan had realized he was trapped between the steering wheel and his seat, it was too late. Mac was out of the stolen Hummer and swinging a gas can as he walked towards Dan's car. Mac upended the gas can and set it on the roof, pouring gas in the hole of the sunroof. With his arms trapped, Dan Westbrook could do nothing except stare at the rearview mirror in horror. With gas flowing all over him, he watched Mac back away and shoot a flare gun straight through where the back window had been, igniting the entire car into a raging inferno. Dan's screams were muffled by the sound of the blaze and the suck of the fire burning oxygen.

Mac had called the Cab Co. he had ready on his cell when he first saw Dan pull up, and now he started the trek back to the address he had given the dispatch for a pick up point. The taxi was pulling up as Mac arrived to the house. He got in and instructed the driver to go to a location a mile away from where he was parked. On the way out of the neighborhood, they were passed by police and fire rescue whirling away with their sirens and flying to the scene at breakneck speeds, determined to save the day.

"It's the same anywhere you go. Always trouble on Saturday night," said the cabbie.

"Yeah, that's why I don't watch the news anymore. Seems like something bad is always happening to good people," replied Mac.

Archer woke from a deep sleep with the ringing of the phone. It was 12:30 AM and there was no way was this going to be good news.

"Archer," he answered.

"Archer, its Jane. Dan Westbrook's been murdered."

100

"What? Murdered?"

"Yeah, someone turned his Mercedes Sedan into a compact with him in it, then roasted him alive," Jane said. "We're trying to track down his ex in Savannah now. She has their son, Bobby."

"Man, I can't believe it, I just ta…Jane, where's Thomas Reynolds right now?"

"In Las Vegas, why?"

"And his girlfriend, Darla Davis?"

"You mean his wife. They were married last night; that's where Dan was returning from."

"Jane, there's something else you should know."

"What is it?"
"Dan called me and asked me to run a check on Darla Davis."

"Why?" asked Jane.

"He said something wasn't right about her, so I had Doc do some digging and she came up clean. In fact, Doc used the words, 'almost too clean.' He didn't want to speculate until he could look a little more."

"Isn't that what you pay him to do?"

"Yes, but Doc is very thorough. He'll make damn sure he's right before he draws any conclusions, and I know he will because he hasn't been wrong yet...ever. How fresh is the crime scene?" asked Archer.

"Pristine. We're waiting on the crime scene photographer now. He was up at Lake Lanier. He's on his way."

"I'm on my way, too, and I don't want to hear any jurisdictional nonsense from the boys. My firm was in charge of their security," barked Archer.

"I wouldn't say that too loud. This guy's a crispy critter."

"Ouch."

"You'll be fine, Handsome. It's my investigation."

"Thanks, Lieutenant Yummy. I'll see you soon."

CHAPTER 14

Mr. and Miss. Thomas Reynolds were in the Presidential Suite at the Bellagio Hotel. They had just come back from gambling on the casino floor, and Thomas was on top of the world. Darla was bored and not on top of anything. It was all she could do to keep the charade up. She wanted to just kill him now. His Southern charm was starting to wear on her.

Just a few more weeks.

Thomas was pouring a glass of malted scotch when the phone rang. "Helloo," Thomas sang.

"Thomas, its Archer. I hate to ruin your Wedding Weekend like this but something terrible has happened. Thomas, Dan Westbrook was killed a little while ago."

"Dan? But how? What do you mean?"

"I don't know all of the details yet, I'm driving there now. All I really know is he is dead, and it was murder. I'll call you as soon as I know what happened."

"Archer, I'm coming home right now."

When she heard the name Archer it more than peaked Darla's attention. She was starting to shake. *Calm down, goddammit.*

"There's no reason to fly home in the middle of the night; there's nothing we can do right now anyway. We have to see exactly what happened first, and that's going to take some time."

"I'm in Las Vegas, Archer," Thomas boomed. "It's always the middle of the night or never the middle of the night, whichever the hell it is, it doesn't matter. I'm coming home NOW!" and he slammed the phone down hard making Darla jump. She had never seen him like this.   He was babbling and storming around the suite. She thought about the 38 in her handbag. Since they flew in the company jet, she was able to bring it.

"What happened, Thomas?" she said in a fake sweet voice.

"Oh, I'm sorry, Darla. Dan Westbrook was killed tonight, and we have to go home. I didn't mean to scare you; I'm just shocked that this could happen. Where was Archer on this one?"

"Who?"

"Oh, Jon Archer does some security work for our firm," Thomas said smugly.

"He works for you," asked Darla.

"In a manner of speaking, yes. We're a client of his."

Thomas picked up his cell phone and dialed a number and put it to his ear. "Paul, we're leaving. Have the jet ready in twenty minutes," ordered Thomas.

Four and a half hours later they would be wheels down at Peachtree DeKalb Airport.

CHAPTER 15

Archer picked up Brody at his house about an hour after leaving his home. Brody lived on Briarcliff Road, very near where Dan did. He had an old Victorian place that was full of antique furniture. It looked like the exact opposite of the kind of place a guy like Brody would live. It looked like a place right out of the 1800s, with lots of hand carved dark woods, felt covered chairs and sofas and little bitsy tables with small doilies on them. He never used any of it; in fact he stayed not in the Master bedroom with an old poster bed and gas heater all on big thick oval rug that reminded him of a cookie, but in the side guest room that had a door leading out to the wrap around porch. He said the place reminded him of his Grandmother's house; he wasn't allowed to touch anything there either. At a quarter till two in the morning when Archer got there, Brody was out back standing in his yard wearing a cowboy hat and boxer shorts, pouring water from a hose into a grill with big bellows of steam mushroom clouding up over his head. He was barbequing. He said he was hungry and couldn't sleep, so he cracked a beer and started up the grill.

"Let's go, Fat Man," Archer said as he was rounding the corner of the porch. Brody used to weigh around 300 pounds, and he was only 5'6". He gained a ton of weight after leaving the military. Not anymore. He was a fit, 210 pound stump. He worked it all off pumping iron in an old boxing gym on the south side.

"I'm ready, Boss, I couldn't sleep for shit anyway" Brody replied.

"I just can't believe this, shit?" whispered Brody after Archer filled him in on what he knew.

"I can't either, but it's happening, and Reynolds is flying back right now from Vegas the night after his wedding – and he is pissed off."

"He got hitched?"

"Yeah, don't get me started on that."

When they pulled up to Dan's street corner, the first thing Archer noticed was that the air smelled like Brody's grill.

It was a hot, thick summer night and the air tasted like a combination of burning hair and overcooked ham and the layer of greasy stench that covered the whole block made you want to shower. The neighbors were still out in the thick of it, gawking in their robes and night curlers, choosing not to dress for the entertainment.

Archer approached the black charred frame of the Benz and peered through the driver's side window. Dan Westbrook looked like he was frozen in time; it reminded Archer of one of those curled up corpses dug up from the remains of Pompeii. Except Dan didn't have the luxury of being flash roasted. He burned alive slowly for several minutes before the gas tank blew. His head, with an open mouthed grimace, was still turned to the rearview mirror. He saw it coming.

From the condition of the inside of the car, Archer knew it was all for the coroner. All the evidence inside, if there was any, had been destroyed.

So Archer backtracked from the side of Dan's car to the driver's door of the Hummer, scouring the ground with a flashlight. Right on the edge of the grass line and the driveway, he spotted a very small white ball. He pulled a pen out of his jacket and stooped down real close and moved it with the pen. It was a wad of chewing gum. He pulled a plastic baggie from his pocket and stuck the pen into the wad and secured it inside. Upon examination, Archer noticed it smelled really bad. He couldn't place his finger on the smell. Then it hit him: nicotine. It was nicotine gum for people trying to quit smoking. He walked and scoured the perimeter of the Hummer fanning back into larger circles until he reached the curb on the other side of the road. When he looked down, he saw a small pool of water and two more wads of gum. *They were parked right here, waiting.*

He picked up the wads with his pen and in the bag they went. Jane saw him stoop down and put something in his pocket.

"Hey, Archer, you wouldn't be disrupting the integrity of my crime scene would you?" she asked.

"I wouldn't dream of it Lieutenant," he said with a smile. "I'm way beyond the tape line, Ma'am."

"What were you putting in your pocket?" she asked.

"Probably nothing, but I'll let you know if it turns out to be anything, and you know I'll share any information I have, if it's germane to the case."

"See that you do, Handsome," Jane said as she walked over to the M.E.

They poked around searching for a couple of more hours.

"Brody, let's ride. I don't want to see Reynolds until we have something for him," he whispered. As they were walking back towards his truck, he brushed against Jane's backside, looking over his shoulder and giving her a wink. She just smiled and shook her head. Archer realized they were in a good place, and they were loving every minute of the flirtatious banter.

"Did you find anything?" Archer asked Brody in the truck.

"I went all around the house and also around the block. I got nothing."

"Well, either they had someone follow them or they got a ride out of here another way. Tomorrow we'll check with the cab companies that service the area."

"Boss, these are serious fucking guys," Brody said, looking straight ahead with a solemn look on his face.

"So are we, Big Boy. So are we."

CHAPTER 16

Thomas hadn't said a word on the trip back to Atlanta. His mind was far away as he stared out into the night at the twinkling lights below, and as his eyes raced over the sporadic gray clouds. He was thinking of days long past when he was young and virile, chumming around campus with his fraternity brothers, Dan and Peter. No one was going to stop the three of them in their endeavor to take the world by the balls and squeeze until all of their hopes and dreams were realized, and no one did – until now.

"Are you alright, Thomas?" asked Darla.

"Yes, yes. I was just remembering Dan and wondering how Peter is doing. He didn't answer when I tried him."

"I'm so sorry for you ...and Peter," Darla said, trying her best to sound sincere.

When they touched down, they de-boarded,

and Paul pulled the limo around. He was Thomas's driver as well. He figured that since it was probably easier for a personal pilot to take a second job as the personal driver than it would be for the personal driver to take a second job as a personal pilot, he might as well take advantage of that.

They rode to the house in Dunwoody in silence, shuffled inside, and went straight to bed. Darla lied in bed and went over their plan from beginning to end, including the audible that had to be called on Dan Westbrook. She tried to anticipate any scenario that could produce obstacles between her and Mavis and their goal. Just as she started to fall asleep, she woke with a sudden jerk. All she could remember was the image in her mind of the black silhouette of her stepfather in the threshold of her bedroom door. She tried to go back to sleep, but couldn't get the thoughts out of her head of the violent sessions of abuse that had plagued her childhood. The physical pain of the weekly, sometimes daily, assault soon vanished, leaving only the mental anguish that would haunt her for the rest of her life. What really broke Lydia Crane and turned her from a fun, sweet happy little girl into an emotionless homicidal zombie was when she found out that her mother knew all along what had been happening to her and acted as if nothing was wrong. Her mother had sacrificed her as an offering to the beast to appease his lust in exchange for room and board. Lydia learned this one hot afternoon by overhearing a conversation between them at the age of sixteen and left home that day never to return.

When Darla woke the next morning, Thomas wasn't there. She slipped on a robe and went downstairs. As she was walking through the huge front room, she saw Thomas sitting at his desk in his library. He looked up at her with a concerned look on his face.

"Darla, would you come in here for a moment. There's something I want to talk to you about." he asked.

Darla felt the grip of fear constrict in her chest. "Good morning," she said as she walked in smiling.

"Oh. Good morning."

The pressure in her chest eased a bit

"Darla, in light of what happened to Dan Westbrook. It got me thinking," Thomas said without looking at her.

'Thinking about what, Dear?"

The pressure was back.

"Well, we had a clause in our company charter that stipulated that if one of the three partners dies, his share of the company stock reverts back to the surviving partners. It was in effort to see that as long as we lived, one of us three would always run the company, not by one of our relatives who would drive the business into the ground. Dan was murdered, so I have to take into consideration that something like that could happen to me. If it did, then all I would be able to leave you would be this house and the beach house in Dunedin, Florida. Everything else – the cars, the jet, all the stock – is all in the company's name. That's why I drew up this bill of sale. It is a binding agreement that says I sold you my share of the stock for $1.00 before I died, but you can't manage it or touch it until I do. I will leave it signed and dated in the safe here at home, and I've just faxed a copy to our attorney. So, by selling out to you before I died, then the stock doesn't revert back to Peter. He is extremely wealthy, he doesn't spend money, he saves it, and he's not in good health anyway. It all boils down to who gets what after we three are gone, and I didn't want you to be pushed out of the picture by ex-wives."

"Why, Thomas…I don't know what to say."

"Say OK. And you owe me a dollar," Thomas said smiling.

"Okay," she said as he was getting up and coming around the desk walking toward her with a naughty look in his eye.

"I'm thinking I might need a little something else besides that dollar," he said, still stalking towards her as she backed up. He lunged for her as she turned to run away shrieking with laughter as he gave chase. It was easy for Darla to have fun with Thomas even if she didn't care about him one iota, because all she had to do was think about all that money and she was instantly in a good mood. Even in bed, while he was grunting away on top of her, she would close her eyes and think of the money and of Mavis, and nothing else seemed to matter.

Later that day, Darla was unpacking some of her things from a box she had gotten from the hotel when she checked out; she had bought all new things since she had been staying at Thomas's house. She picked up the jacket to the suit she wore out of prison and the bus locker key fell to the floor. When she bent down and picked it up, she paused. An idea came to her, and she wanted to call Mavis right away.

The voice on the other end said to go to the Dunk-N-Dine on Roswell road at two o' clock on Monday. Darla arrived at 2 PM sharp, driving a nice Lexus that was a wedding gift from Thomas. She went inside and sat at the counter. She was going over the idea in her head when someone approached her from behind.

"Cock -a-doodle doo," she heard from behind her.

It was Mavis, dressed to the nines in a navy blue suit. "Let's grab a booth," Mavis said, smiling from ear to ear.

They went to the back and sat down, ordered coffee and huddled up. Mavis pulled out a flask and made the coffees Irish. Lydia told Mavis about how Thomas and Peter ended up with Dan's stock because of the clause in the charter and how Thomas sold his share to her, so now they needed to have Peter killed. That way by the time they killed Thomas, they would have all of their stocks and would have double their money, minus a couple of points.

Mavis was proud of Lydia for coming up with this amendment to the plan.

"Nice job, baby. That extra cash will go a long way in Bangkok. I can't wait to get there, and we can kick back with no worries ever again. OK, I'll call Mac, and we'll get this show on the road."

"It's all going to work out, right, Mavis?" Lydia asked, looking worried.

"Of course," Mavis said with her arm around

her. "Baby, it's our time."

CHAPTER 17

Since they had a couple days' down time waiting for the lab report results from the evidence collected in Dan's driveway, and other than a couple of errands he may or may not run later, Archer and Jane were making dinner on the back porch at the ranch. It was a beautiful summer evening, with a red and purple streaked sun sinking over the pastures behind the house. The lightning bugs were just starting to get frisky out over the garden. Archer was rolling a thick marinated Chateau Briand across the grill and tending to a couple of foil wrapped ears of corn down in the coals. They had polished off the better part of a large bottle of Burgundy and were enjoying an evening off, dancing around to Van Morrison and laughing at Jimmy, who was being made a fool of by a young cottontail in the field. Jane went back inside to wash the salad and was standing in front of the window over the sink looking at Archer when it suddenly shattered and she was looking square at the business end of a long grain bullet. She jumped backward and fell on her butt. Archer yelled to Jimmy, "Get 'em, boy!" Jimmy was trained to run toward gunfire. When he was on the move zigging and zagging, no one could lay a sight nor scope on him.

Archer ran through the open sliding glass door, knocking the closed screen door right off the hinges, sending it flying through the living room. He dove into the kitchen and crawled with his elbows to Jane who was sitting up looking at the window. "Are you hit?" he yelled.

"No, the bullet didn't penetrate the glass. See? It's still wedged in there. But it scared the shit out of me."

"Follow me," he said, still elbowing across the floor with great speed. Jane was right behind him. They got past the windows and jumped up and went around through the study and up the stairs. At the end of the hall was a big gray steel door. Archer punched a four-digit code on the pad in the hall as he ran by, and it swung opened. He shoved Jane inside, grabbed a 45 service piece that was Velcroed to the wall by the door, and ran out. He could hear Jane as the door swung closed, "Wait! You're not leaving me in here. I'm a police off…" When the door slammed shut, Archer punched in a five-digit code and ran down the stairs.

By the time he ran back outside, less than a minute had passed. He could hear Jimmy barking way down in the lower back field. He jumped in his truck and tore off down the path, running along the fence line heading to the back of the property; he could still hear Jimmy barking. He grabbed his cell phone and called the phone in the panic room. "Hello?" Jane said.

"Jane, listen."

"Archer, you bastard!"

"Listen to me: I need you there to be my eyes. Now turn the red switch to the wall of monitors on."

"Ok, I got it."

"What do you see?"

"Jimmy. He's chasing somebody to the back fence. There's a truck waiting on the other side of the road. Now they're over the fence, and they just jumped in the truck... rolling up the window, Jimmy's trying to get to them. They've started the truck, and it's rolling, Jimmy's chasing them – oh crap, Jimmy just jumped in the back of the truck!"

"Shit!" Archer said as he threw the phone down and pulled a Rockford slide on the two worn spots in the grass that indicated the road. He started heading back the way he came. He roared down the path to the dirt driveway, flew up over the cattle guard, and took off in the direction the truck went. He could've only gone one way because the other way led to an open pasture. After about a mile, he saw Jimmy lying on the side of the road and new disturbances in the road from where someone slammed on the brakes, then spun the tires, speeding up. He did a power slide sideways and came to a halt in the middle of the road. He ran over to Jimmy, who really looked bad; there were big bloody spots on him where he slid on the pavement at a high rate of speed, and he couldn't seem to focus his eyes.

"You'll be alright, boy. I got you," he said

softly as he picked Jimmy up in his arms.

He drove back to the house, ran in, let Jane out of the panic room, and then grabbed a stack of towels from the linen closet.

"I gotta go. Jimmy's in bad shape. I'm taking him to Dr. Fortenberry's house. Go to the address book in my desk in the study and call him; tell him we're on the way," he said to Jane, his voice quivering.

"Got it. Now go on and hurry," Jane said.

Archer gave her a one-armed squeeze and a quick kiss and ran out the door.

She called Dr. Fortenberry and explained what had happened to Jimmy. He said he would be waiting, and they should bring him around behind the house to the examination room. She thanked them and called Archer.

"Hello," Archer answered in a loud voice.

"Doc Fortenberry said to take Jimmy to the back whe…."

"I'm way ahead of you. Thanks I'll be back soon, I hope," he said as he hung up. He was carrying Jimmy from the truck to the exam room moving fast. The nurse saw him coming through the glass and jumped up and opened the door for them. She stood staring outside after they passed through looking at Archer's truck. It was parked on a sign that read examination room and there were two wide tire tracks from where he made a bee line from the road to the door. The roped off patch holding the azalea beds were trenched and there was a pile of broken pieces of dog and cat statues that were casualties of Archer's haste as well.

Jane went to the kitchen and poured a big glass of scotch and a separate glass of water. Then she went out to the back porch and poured the glass of water over the smoking burnt tenderloin and black foil wrapped corn on the grill and took a long swig from the scotch.

She went back inside and inspected the bullet that was lodged in the window over the sink. It was a high caliber round that was stopped cold by the protected glass. She went out to her car, grabbed her bag, and brought it back inside. She took out a baggie, some gloves, a ruler, and a camera, and went to work. She photographed the window set with and without the ruler held up beside it and then removed the bullet and put it in the evidence bag. She pulled a laser pen out of her pocket and threaded it through the hole at the precise angle of the bullet penetration. She grabbed her binoculars out of her bag and went to the back porch. When she found the red spot from the laser, she could see that it was the same spot that she and Archer found the cigarette butts.

Archer went back to the house without Jimmy; the vet said they would have to keep him there overnight. He had three broken ribs and had lost a lot of blood. He had a concussion too.

Archer found Jane in his study on the phone.

"How's Jimmy?" she asked.

He filled her in on Jimmy's condition, then she showed him the laser path and the bullet. He pulled an evidence bag out of the drawer that had one of the wads of gum in it and handed it to Jane.

"Its nicotine gum from in front of Dan's house. Maybe you can extract some DNA out of it. I wanted to give it to you last night but I wanted you to be alone. That way you can introduce it whenever you want to, but right now I need to go interview Peter and find out if he can tell me anything he might not have told you guys and see if anyone in Dan's life was trying to kick the habit. Will you wait for me?"

"Thanks, Archer," she said sarcastically. "I should arrest you for withholding evidence, and, if you're lucky, I'll be here when you get back. I want to know what Peter tells you."

"Lock the doors after I leave. The code for the panic room is 1010. Anyone comes by to pay us a visit, you use it. It's the best vantage point anyway, and you can see the whole ranch, so don't try and be the Lone Ranger. "

"Deal," answered Jane.

CHAPTER 18

Peter Westbrook hadn't come out of his house all weekend. His heart had been deteriorating long before the tragedy of his brother's murder ever happened. His kitchen counter looked like a pharmacy due to the 40 or so prescription bottles strewn everywhere, and he had a portable heart monitor beside his bed where he convalesced. His bed was covered in stacks of magazines, newspapers and books, the majority of which were published by Reynolds Enterprises, with a small bare spot on the top edge where he laid. He would have to leave the house tomorrow for the funeral and he didn't know where the energy or desire would come from.

He lived in a house in Dunwoody, not far from the Reynolds house, right on the Chattahoochee River. The entire west side of the house was covered in glass, giving a spectacular view of the river from any room facing that direction. There was a wide two level back porch with big wicker chairs and a table with an umbrella on the bottom and two smaller chairs upstairs that were right outside Peter's bedroom door. He would lie in bed and watch the dark green water roll by like an endless parade of time, which was a constant reminder of how it marches on no matter what.

Thomas had come by to talk about what Dan would have wanted and some loose ends that needed to be tied up after a partner dies unexpectedly. Anything that jeopardized the financial sovereignty of the corporation was dealt with in a timely manner. After they finished talking, it was 8 PM, and Peter excused himself to take his medicine

As he walked to the kitchen to get one his nitroglycerin tablets, the phone rang. He had let it go to voicemail for the last couple of days and had many messages, largely condolence calls, but as he was passing by while it was ringing, he noticed the caller ID light up and display the words, JON ARCHER. He picked up the handset and sat down on a stool in the kitchen by the phone. "Yes," said Peter in a feeble voice.

"Peter, this is Archer. I need to talk with you if you feel up to it. I'm trying to find out what happened to Dan."

"I know the feeling. Thomas and I were just discussing that, but I'm not sure how I can be of any help to you."

"Well, I'm not either really, but sometimes the smallest little things end up being important. Is Thomas there with you now?" asked Archer.

"Yes. He came by to discuss some business matters."

"Listen, I'm nearby in Roswell. Do you mind if I swing by for a few minutes and talk with both of you?"

"No, no, by all means, Jon. I'll do anything I can to help you catch the son of a bitch."

"Great. I'll be by in a little while."

"Fine, when you get here just come on in. Thomas and I are upstairs," Peter answered and hung up.

Archer made a mental note to talk to Peter about leaving his doors unlocked under the recent circumstances.

Peter went back and sat on the side of his bed and felt the dull pain in his chest that he'd grown accustomed to and remembered that he had forgotten to get the nitro tabs in the kitchen; Archer's phone call drew him off of his task.

"Damn, I forgot my meds. By the way, Jon Archer is coming by; he'll be here in a few minutes."

Thomas was standing in front of the big window looking out at the river. There was a fog riding the water about three feet from the surface, and sticking out of it was a man in a Gheenew. He was fishing for rainbows and browns and the like in the shadows, and the darkness was setting in. Thomas returned to the chair by the bed, picked up the newspaper, and he noticed he was struggling to see. As he drew the curtains and turned on the light, he saw that the fisherman had left and given up for the day. He wondered if they were biting on such a warm summer night.

When Peter returned to the kitchen, he heard a noise coming from the side of the house. Sounded like twigs breaking, he thought.

"Archer, is that you?" he called through the open window and into the darkness.

No answer.

Then the sound of splintering wood and shattering glass thundered through the kitchen as the side door leading out to the driveway came exploding off the frame and went smashing into the breakfast table. Peter dropped his pill bottle, and they sprayed across the floor. Thomas ran into the kitchen a second or two later yelling "What the hell is going on?" and then he was shot right between the eyes by a small caliber handgun from a large man standing in the kitchen wearing black clothes. As a small trickle of blood ran down the confused face of Thomas Reynolds, he fell to his knees and subsequently forward, onto his face. As Peter watched in horror, he saw the figure of the large man rushing towards him, and then everything went black.

When Peter came to, he was sitting upright with his hands bound and duct tape wrapped around his mouth.

Mac was sitting in front of Peter, slapping his face.

"Wakie, wakie," Mac said.

Peter looked at him, frozen in fear.

"I just have one question. Your answer won't make any difference what happens to you. You're gonna die tonight. Sorry about that, but it may make a difference to whether or not I kill one of your boys or both. See I need to know what you know about what happened to your brother. What have the police found out about what happened to Dan or that little security team of your company's? Do you understand what I'm asking here, Petey?"

Peter nodded furiously.

"Ok, I'm gonna take this tape off. No screaming, no begging, just answers. Are we clear?"

Again Peter nodded.

As Mac ripped the tape off in a fast jerk, Peter let out one of those internal yelps that you do when your mouth is closed.

"Look, I swear to you I don't know anything, neither do the police or anyone else. Jon Archer is on his way here to ask me questions because they don't know anything either."

"Archer's coming here tonight?" asked Mac.

Peter nodded.

"Well, Petey. You may have just saved your boys, but you understand this; if you're lying to me about any of this, then I'll have to pay them both a visit, and it won't be quick like you – it'll be really nasty."

"I understand. I swear, I'm not lying," Peter said with sincerity.

"OK, then. Any last words?" he said as he turned on the defibrillator.

Peter could hear the charging tone rise to a high squeal until the green light came on and looked at Mac. Then he looked down at the two wires strung from the unit to two contacts taped to his chest.

"Our Father, who art in heaven, hallo…"

Mac rolled his eyes and turned the switch, cutting him off mid-sentence.

"I hate it when they pray," Mac said out loud.

CHAPTER 19

The machine stopped Peter's heart in one painful, wrenching spasm. Mac got up and turned the lights off everywhere in the house and used the light of the refrigerator to start cleaning up when he saw the headlights from Archer's car shine across the kitchen. Mac ran out the door hole. When Archer walked to the side door to come in, it took a minute to realize the door was lying splintered on the table, and not just open. He saw Peter strapped to the chair and Thomas lying face down in a dried pool of blood and heard a small outboard engine turn over. He ran back outside and around to the dock and saw the shadow of a boat moving away. Then, he saw a brief flash in the fog, like someone snapped a picture, and then something hit him in the shoulder and knocked him down.

I've been shot! I never heard it. The flash must have been a gun firing, but I never heard it. Man, they were right, you never hear the ones that get you!

He picked himself up from the grass, already wet from the dew, and ran back inside, taking the pulse of both Peter Westbrook and Thomas Reynolds. They were both dead. He grabbed a handful of napkins off the counter, wadded them up in a ball, and held it against his shoulder. Then he took the duct tape off the counter, holding it carefully in a napkin, and wrapped the roll around and around his shoulder until it was tight, then tore it and put it back on the counter. He called Jane to send an ambulance and the parade.

Other than the two dead guys, nothing else seemed amiss except the side door in the kitchen that had seen better days.

Jane had officers escort Archer to the hospital so they could expedite his treatment. The doctors stitched him up and gave him some antibiotics and vicodin and recommended he go home and go to bed; they would schedule him to see a specialist to decide if he would need surgery. Archer made Brody pick him up at the hospital and take him back to Peter's house.

Reluctantly, Brody obliged, and they were there in minutes.

"Archer, what the hell are you doing back here?" Jane asked with blatant exasperation.

"I just want to look around. I didn't exactly have time to earlier."

"This entire area is a crime scene, Archer. You can't go traipsing through here, and you know that."

"Yes, and part of that crime was me getting shot. I think I've earned a little leeway," explained

Archer.

"OK, come on. But don't touch a thing," she warned as she led Archer back into the kitchen through the missing door. "CSI is finishing up, and the M.E. is going to take the bodies to the morgue." She pointed at Peter, "That one will have to have an autopsy, and that one – well it's pretty clear what killed him," she finished, pointing at Thomas.

"He was a surprise," Archer said nodding toward Thomas. "Peter was the target. I spoke to him around 8 PM to tell him I wanted to come by; he said Thomas had stopped by to go over some things about Dan. Whoever killed Peter didn't know Thomas was here. It wouldn't take long, even for an amateur to realize Peter was always at home. So the guy comes in and surprises the shit out of Peter; hence, the busted-in door and pills everywhere. Next, Thomas comes in to see what all the noise is about and gets killed on reflex. Then the killer starts to gather up his supplies," Archer points to the duct tape, "and I surprise him when I pull up. So before he can finish, he runs around back." Archer walks out and around the back corner of the house, Jane and Brody in tow, and points at the dock.

"That's when he jumped in his john boat. I came running up, and he shot me and disappeared in the fog."

"Nice job, Archer," Jane said then looked at Brody, who just shrugged.

"It also occurred to me that this happened just over an hour after someone took a shot at you at my house," Archer said.

"Someone shot at you?" Brody asked Jane.

"Yeah. If Archer wasn't so paranoid and didn't have bullet proof windows, I'd be toast right now," Jane admitted.

"I told you, Boss. This guy's serious," Brody added.

"Yeah, that's the problem."

"OK, I'll bite," Jane said.

"Well, this guy is serious; he's serious like a pro. He's got supplies, exit strategies, and information. Which begs the question: who hired him and why?"

"Have you told the new wife, Darla Davis, about any of this?" asked Archer.

"Not yet. I am going there when I leave here," answered Jane.

"Good. Brody and I will go with you," Archer added.

CHAPTER 20

Jane knocked on the Reynolds door around 3 AM. The porch light came on, and a housekeeper answered the door wearing a robe asking why they had come at such an odd hour. She was an old black woman with big beautiful eyes and a wide smile that made you feel warm. All three of them noticed that it was almost like she was expecting them, and she was glad they were there.

"Ma'am, I'm Lieutenant Kincaid with the Atlanta Police Department, and these are two of my colleagues. We need to speak to Darla Reynolds please, it's urgent," Jane said in an official tone.

"Just a minute, Honey," she replied and started to close the door, then she recognized Archer.

"Is that you Mr. Jon?"

"Yes, Minnie it's me. How are you?"

"Well I'm OK, considering what happened to Mr. Dan. I'm sure ya'll being here this late and Mr. Thomas gone, this ain't gonna be good news either, is it?"

"No, Ma'am, it's not. Let us talk to Miss Reynolds, and then you and I will talk."

"OK, Mr. Jon."

A few minutes later, Darla came downstairs, confused and sleepy, and asked the three of them into the parlor. She asked Minnie to bring some coffee.

"Miss Reynolds, I'm afraid we have some bad news. Thomas Reynolds and Peter Westbrook were killed earlier this evening at Peter's house," Jane explained.

"What? I mean, he went to Peter's to discuss some business matters after dinner. You're telling me they are both dead? Who would want to hurt Thomas?" she asked.

"At this point we're not sure he was the target. It looks like he was just at the wrong place at the wrong time," Jane said studying Darla's face.
Darla managed to squeeze out a few tears and asked if they were sure it was Thomas.

"Yes. This is Jon Archer. He runs a security firm that sometimes handles internal problems with Reynolds Enterprises, and he identified the bodies."

"I just can't believe this is happening. We just got married this weekend, the day before yesterday in fact…in Las Vegas."

Archer was reading her body language and was convinced she was lying about something. He saw a familiarity about her, but dismissed it as seeing her picture when Dan faxed it over to him at his office.

"Darla, can you think of anyone who might want to harm Thomas or Peter?" asked Jane.

"No, not anyone. I didn't really know Peter that well, but Thomas was the kindest man I have ever met."

Minnie brought in a tray of cups and a pot of coffee and set it on the table between them.

"Thank you, Minnie," Darla said to the house-keeper with a smile. Jane noticed that she didn't smile back; in fact it looked like she rolled her eyes.

"Mrs. Reynolds, did Thomas ask you to sign a prenuptial agreement before you two were married?" Archer asked.

Brody and Jane shot him a look.

"No, he did not. I suggested we sign one because I wanted him to know that I didn't care about his money," Darla answered glaring at Archer.

"Did you sign one?"

"Yes, he had one drawn up and we signed it together at his office the day we left for Vegas."

Jane was furiously taking notes.

Brody asked what the agreement stipulated.

"Just that if the marriage ended in divorce, we both left with what we came with," Darla said with another tear.

"Thomas did draw up another agreement when he found out Dan had been killed that sold me his share of Reynolds stock. He said he didn't want me left out since the company owned most all of his assets."

"Do you have a copy of both agreements?" asked Jane.

"Yes, the prenup is in a file upstairs, and the bill of sale for the stock is in the safe. I'll get it for you," Darla said as she got up and went upstairs.

"What do you guys think?" Jane asked.

"She's lying," Brody said

"Or, at the very least, she's hiding something," Archer added.

"What makes you so sure?"

"Three reasons," Archer said. "One, we have been extensively trained at reading people's body language. Two, she seems more concerned about helping us than she does that her husband was just murdered, and three…." He looked at Brody.

"She didn't ask how he was killed, which is usually the first thing they ask, it satisfies their morbid curiosity" Brody chimed in.

"I see your point," said Jane.

They heard water running and dishes rattling around in the kitchen.

"I'll be right back," Archer said as he stood and hurried towards where they heard the noise come from.

Archer walked in the kitchen, which was as big as most apartments, and said to Minnie as she was standing at the sink, "Excuse me, Minnie, what do you make of all this mess?"

"Lord, Mr. Jon, I don't know. I heard the police lady say that Mr. Reynolds and the other Mr. Westbrook were killed. I declare, seems like all these men are dying, and the only thing different 'round here is her," she nodded over her shoulder, indicating Darla.

"Thanks, Minnie," Archer said and walked out.

Darla came back downstairs with the file containing their birth certificates and other important documents, including the prenup.

"I don't have the combination to the safe. That's where the bill of sale is," Darla said as Archer walked back to the couch. She looked back where Archer had come from and heard Minnie in the kitchen. They saw the look on her face change from fake sadness to worry.

"That's OK. If it's official, then his attorney

will have a copy," Archer said.

"I'd like to be alone now. I don't feel so good," Darla said putting her hand on her chest like she was saying the Pledge of Allegiance.

"Thank you, Mrs. Reynolds. Here's my card. Please call me if you remember anything, anything at all," Jane said, shoving a business card in her hand.

Darla showed them out, and on the way to the car Archer said, "Here's my card? Call me if you remember anything. Who are you? Colombo!"

"Bite me, Archer," Jane replied.

"I would if we could ever have a normal date; I want a rain check on the Chateau Briand dinner."

Archer noticed Jane was staring at his chest; he had a moment of flattery before he looked down and saw the big blood stain on his shoulder that had run down and soaked the shirt on his chest.

Brody saw it at the same time.

"Boss, I'm taking you home. Your stitches are busting up."

"No, I got this Brody. I'll take him home," Jane said.

Archer shot Brody a look as if he were the teacher's pet.

"Where do you guys stand on the funeral to-morrow?" Jane asked.

"We wouldn't miss it for the world," Archer

answered.

"You might have to miss it if you're bleeding to death. Let's go, Archer. Goodnight, Brody, we'll see you tomorrow."

"Brody, find out if there was nicotine gum in that trash at Peter's house or on the lawn from the side door around to the back at the dock, I want to tie the two crime scenes together. Also, go back when the fog has lifted and see if there are any businesses on the other side of the river. They might have cameras," Archer said.

"Boss, I got this. I know what to do. I'll report to you tomorrow at the funeral," Brody said in an understanding voice.

On the way home, Archer made Jane stop and wake up Dr. Fortenberry to check on Jimmy. Luckily, he was already up. Jimmy had responded to the antibiotics and could go home to finish recuperating.

When they got to the ranch, Jane took Jimmy in and put him in his bed in front of the fireplace, then helped Archer in and wrapped him in fresh bandages, depositing him on the couch. As she turned to go upstairs and shower, she saw Archer on the couch with no shirt and bandages on his chest and Jimmy in his bed looking exactly the same way. She shook her head and said, "Miss Virginia, look after them a while. I have to go freshen up."

After a shower, she put on one of Archers T-shirts and nestled in beside him on the couch. He mumbled something in his sleep about jurisdiction and pulled her in close and started snoring. She soon followed suit.

CHAPTER 21

On the morning before the day of the funeral, Mavis went shopping for some items they would need and met Darla at a motel. They put together some specific items in a new briefcase. First, it was two dossiers, one on each of the Westbrook brothers, complete with bios and pictures. They also typed a letter on the computer and included it with the bus locker key.

Mavis put the briefcase in Harlan's path later that afternoon by placing it in the foyer of his drug dealer's building right before he walked in. She knew he would be coming by that afternoon; Harlan came by every afternoon because he could never afford more than a day's supply at any one time. Harlan saw it when he walked in and decided not to pick it up after looking around and went up to the his dealer's apartment. Less than ten minutes later he came back down, high. It was still there and, after looking around again, he snatched it up and went home.

When Harlan got home his father was asleep, so he sat at his kitchen table, cooked up his new supply, and loaded a big shot for his arm. His guy only gave him a taste at his house and told him to bang it up at home if he wanted more. He tied his bicep off with an old necktie that he had never worn, at least not around his neck. He slapped his arm awake and plunged in the steel teat that he needed to feed on. He sat back while a wave of euphoria washed over him, and when his eyes came into focus, he was staring at the briefcase. He pulled it over in front of him and tried to open it. It was locked. He got up and pulled a screwdriver from a kitchen drawer, pried open the case, and inspected the contents. He thumbed through the two files and picked up the letter. This was a letter of solicitation to kill the two brothers for a crime they committed years ago.

Dear Sir,

As we discussed, the files on the subject are enclosed, complete with photos. The sooner you can get this done, the better. As you know, these men raped me back in college and I want them to pay with their lives.

I have enclosed a bus locker key. Once it's been confirmed that they have both been dealt with, you will receive a call on the enclosed phone letting you know that the entire $100,000 has been deposited at the bus station downtown. You can then retrieve your money and leave town.

Miss Pissed Off

Harlan could not believe what he was reading. "Holy Shit!" he exclaimed. "No fucking way! This is an assassin's briefcase. A stupid ass assassin. Is this shit for real?" he mumbled as he was looking through the dossiers and staring at the pictures. "These suit wearin' white chumps don't look like they'd even be a problem at all for me, much less a killer," he said as he took a slug from a bottle of Jim Beam that was sitting on the table and stared down at it all.

Harlan looked over at the TV in the living room. It had Headline News on and the reporter was live on the scene outside the house of a double murder.

"The police won't say whether or not they have any suspects, but sources say this is definitely related to the murder of Dan Westbrook, who was burned alive in his car last Saturday night. Last night, his brother, Peter Westbrook, and the two brothers' business partner, Thomas Reynolds, were killed. I repeat, the three founding partners of Reynolds Enterprises are dead. Their mega million dollar corporation has fallen victim to the worst kind of hostile takeover; this is Michelle Nunez for Headline News."

"That's them!" Harlan shouted. "Those are the suit wearin' white chumps; the stupid ass assassin's already done it!"

Harlan contemplated what this meant for him.

If I keep this stuff, that phone might ring and tell me to go pick up the money. I doubt it would be too risky because surely there's not another briefcase. This could be my one and only chance to get out of here and have enough money for my Pops to go to the old folks home, where he could get the medical attention he needs. And I could take this monkey off my back and kick him in the balls.

Harlan kept pouring over the pages of documents and running through every possible scenario in his head, trying to play devil's advocate to himself. He couldn't find anything wrong with this, provided the phone call came, and, if there were any holes in the plan, he had the proof in the briefcase that he hadn't killed anyone. Worst case, he was taking the opportunity to get paid from bad money and capitalize on a crime someone else had committed. These men were already dead, and that wasn't going to change whether he took advantage of this or not.

CHAPTER 22

At 4 AM on Wednesday morning, a call was placed to the Atlanta Police Department tip line saying that a conversation was overheard in a bar where a guy supposedly took out a couple of businessmen, and he was to pick up the payment at the downtown bus station in a locker. No other information was left on the message and the call was made from a payphone outside a strip club on Piedmont just after they closed. The tip didn't make it to Jane until 7 AM. The call came in on her cell phone. She slipped away from Archer's clutches on the couch and answered the phone. She listened for a minute. "You mean this guy could have already picked up the money?" she said to the Desk Sergeant.

"I suppose. Look, Lieutenant, I just got the latest memos from the overnight tip line a minute ago. I leafed through them, and when I saw it I called you. That's all I know."

"That's alright, Sarge. You did the right thing

calling me," replied Jane.

She called the bullpen at the station and asked for Detective Jackson. "Get your ass down to the bus station and stake out the lockers. We're looking for a perp doing a pickup. We don't know which locker or who is picking up. What we do know is it may be our guy on the Reynolds/Westbrooks murders."

Jane put down her phone and saw that Jimmy was slowly trying to get up. It was obviously time for him to go outside. Jane picked him up in her arms and carried him out. He stood in the grass on weak legs and with an embarrassed look on his face he relived himself. Jane made an effort for Jimmy to see that she wasn't watching, and she looked out over the pasture and saw a big beautiful majestic buck standing on the ridge with the sun coming up behind him. He had a circle of light around him that seemed to come down from the sky in a straight line, as if he had been touched by the finger of God. She wondered how many sights of this enormous beauty went unnoticed because people just didn't take the time to look. She let Jimmy walk beside her back into the house and when she turned to close the door, the buck was gone as if he were never there to begin with.

She showered, dressed, and made some coffee. Then she checked her email on Archer's computer in his study. She was snooping at the pictures on the wall of him in army and police functions and fishing trips with Brody and Doc and decided that Archer was not only the real deal but also the kind of man she needed in her life. She was the daughter of a cop who wanted a son to carry on the family tradition. From an early age, her father had prepared her for the cop's life and, by the time she went to the academy, she was more than ready. She was top of her class and graduated with honors. She retreated back to the front room and slid in under Archer's arm again and fell back asleep.

CHAPTER 23

At 9 AM, Harlan was awakened by an argument between his neighbor, Mr. Mobley, and his sometimes girlfriend. Mr. Mobley was accusing her of whoring around and drinking his liquor. This was not unlike all of the other loud, if not violent, episodes in the past, which happened about twice a week. One instance in particular that especially imposed on Harlan was when he had to go outside in the back of their house and physically pull him off her. Mr. Mobley thought he saw her smile at the pizza delivery kid, and it threw him into a psychotic rage. He was trying to shove pizza down her throat and was doing a pretty good job of it. By the time Harlan pulled him back, she was choking on a huge wad of pizza dough and two of her teeth.

Harlan was quite immune to those feelings himself. He found it easy to control himself when it came to being patient with women and children. Just as he reaffirmed himself as belonging to a better class of people than the likes of Mr. Mobley, the cell phone rang. At first, the sound he was hearing did not register. It was a crude version of Pink Floyd's song "Money." Then he realized what he was hearing was the ill-gotten cell phone from the briefcase and this might be his ticket out of the projects.

He hit the send button and didn't say anything. A voice on the other end said, "Good job. Now leave town. You may want to take a bus," and the line went dead.

Harlan felt something that was foreign to him: hope.

He showered and shaved and paid close attention to his appearance for the first time in as long as he could remember, then slipped on his black socks and church shoes. He pulled his only suit out of a plastic sleeve and dressed quietly so as not wake up his father. He stared at his reflection and was pleased with the results. He hid the briefcase under his bed and set out on his journey to the life he was so sure he deserved.

When he walked through the terminal, he looked nervous. He also had an air about him that gave him a sense of purpose. It was short lived because when he shoved the key into locker 228 and took the satchel out and started back out, he was immediately approached by three detectives and a few uniforms. Later, when he asked what it was that gave him away, they told him that most people either drop off a bag at the lockers and get on a bus or they get off a bus and pick up a bag. Harlan got out of a cab outside and made a bee-line for the locker looking right and left along the way and stopped and did a slow, cautious $360°$ in front of the locker before opening it, making sure he had scanned the room. What he didn't do was take into consideration the eight surveillance cameras trained on the bank of lockers.

Mavis jimmied the back door of Harlan's house and slipped inside with his father on the front porch unaware of anything, much less that someone may be inside. He just kept on waving at the passing cars. It took her about two minutes to find the brilliantly hidden briefcase and she laid it on the bed. She opened it up, and, due to the damaged lock, that was no difficult task. She removed the letter addressed to "Sir" and replaced it with a mission statement that she and Lydia had cooked up and had a ball writing. It declared the white bastards in business suits as the cause of all of his problems. He would strike a blow to those that had ruined his life. It went on and on about how all of the problems of the world were due to the money hungry white men that had benefited from the toil and sweat from working slave men like his ancestors. With a smirk of pride, Mavis exited Harlan's hovel the same way she came.

CHAPTER 24

Jane got a call from Detective Jackson and woke Archer to explain what happened at the bus station, telling him they had Harlan in custody downtown. On the way in, they stopped by Judge Lee's house and had a warrant signed to go search Harlan's home. When they reached the house, Jane told Harlan's father they had a warrant and were going inside.

"He's not home, but go on in. He'll be along soon enough. You're a friend of Harlan's, you can come on in then," he said never stopping waving and not listening to her anyway.

Archer went around back, which was standard procedure in case there were any surprises. He noticed the jimmy marks on the door frame that Mavis had left. Again, it only took a few minutes to find the briefcase and after inspecting the contents, Jane spoke.

"Archer, check this out. This guy was one step away

from being the Unabomber." She read part of the rant and ravings in the manifesto and examined the dossiers. "We have got this guy sewed up," Jane said as she passed the files to Archer.

"It would appear so at first glance," Archer replied as he finished looking around. Jane called the detectives and they came over to comb the place, while the two of them went downtown to have a sit down with Harlan.

Harlan was in interrogation room C and Archer and Jane stood behind the two-way glass and observed him before going in. He was fidgeting around, literally itching for a fix, and he was starting to sweat. The detectives came into the observation room and told Jane and Archer that Harlan had told them that he didn't kill anyone. He said he found the briefcase with a letter to the real killer and he figured the guy lost the case, and he just went to get paid. When Jane and Archer went inside to speak to Harlan, the first thing he asked was if they had found the briefcase.

"Yeah, we found it, Harlan," Jane said.

You could see the relief wash over his face.

"But, there was no letter. Just a mission statement from you to the world professing your hate for Corporate White America," Jane finished.

"What? No, no, no. There was a letter in that case to a hit man to do those guys and instructions on when the money would be put in the locker. All I did was go pick up the bag. I ain't killed nobody," Harlan swore.

He was scared, especially after they let him stew for a while, and he had the chance to think about what Jane told him about what it was like to be gang raped in Reidsville State Penitentiary.

Archer and Jane were behind the glass again.

"I don't know ,"said Archer. "He just doesn't have the look of a killer..."

"We have a first rate case against this guy, Archer. All the evidence points to him. We have to trust the evidence," Jane argued.

"Call it a hunch, but it just doesn't add up. I mean, from what we saw at his house, Harlan is a forger and a doper, but a homicidal killer? That takes a pretty big sack, and this guy's a sniveling little boy. The ranting in that statement doesn't even sound like him, and there were fresh jimmy marks on the back door frame. I believe him. I smell a set up."

Detective Jackson came back in and told them that the D.A s Office was planning to indict Harlan due to the evidence they had on him.

"No surprise there. Let me guess: Edelman signed the indictment?" Archer predicted.

Detective Jackson nodded.

"Not that it would matter to Edelman, but I'm telling you this is not the guy who killed Peter and Thomas and then shot me. The guy who did that was a lot bigger."

"Archer, you said yourself you didn't get a good look at him," Jane argued.

"I didn't because it was dark and foggy, but I saw his general size and his outline and he was a lot bigger than Harlan. I mean I couldn't tell you what his face looks like, but I could see how tall he was."

"Well, until you can come up with some evidence implicating someone else, anyone else, he's our man," Jane said, pointing through the window at Harlan.

CHAPTER 25

Darla walked out of the Reynolds house wearing a black dress and veil, with an attaché case under her arm and big, round dark sunglasses. She waited for Paul to come around and open the door. When he didn't come, she opened the door and got in. As it started pulling away from the house, the partition lowered and Mavis was looking at Lydia through the rearview mirror.

"Cock-a doodle doo," she said.

"Mavis? What the hell are you doing here?" Lydia said in a whispered voice.

"Relax; I'm your driver now."

"Where is Paul?"

"I gave him his walking papers," Mavis said. "Now did you call the attorney's office?" she asked

Lydia.

"Yes, and he didn't mind telling me he thought it was an inappropriate time to do this since we were burying Thomas today. What do you mean his walking papers?"

"I told him his services as the driver would no longer be needed, but to be on standby with the plane and who gives a shit what that asshole attorney thinks anyway. Did he sell the stock and deposit the money?"

"I told him that I couldn't bear being here without Thomas and I was leaving town as soon as possible. I told him to sell the stock and the houses. He said it would be done today and he would email me the account numbers when it was done. We can check it on the laptop," Lydia answered.

Mavis's cell phone rang, and she snatched it up.

"Yeah?" she said into the handset. "I don't care if no one's home. Stay there and keep an eye on the place. I want to know when he gets there. I've got a little surprise for him," Mavis said.

"Who was that?" asked Lydia.

"No one, it's just a little something I have cooked up for that shit heel, Archer."

"Damn. Look, Mavis, I know you said plans have changed, and I should stay away from Archer because the money's more important, but I wish I could be there to fucking kill him myself."

"I have a plan that you will find very satisfying. We need to be far away with a good alibi when Archer meets God, believe me."

"I always have, Mavis," Lydia replied with complete sincerity.

Mavis didn't even bother slowing down when they pulled out past the gate and on to the road. The group of reporters and paparazzi were diving in all directions for safety. One guy tried to stick a microphone in the crack of the driver's window and Mavis snatched it out of his hand and tossed it in the seat beside her and kept on driving.

When they arrived at the funeral, there were a thousand people there, mostly business associates and city officials. Reporters from all over the country, and some others, were swarming in a thick mob that aggregated behind whoever was the most important at the time. Mavis made a hole, and Darla followed through the doors of the church and into the chapel, right down to the front row. Darla gave a stellar performance during the service as the grieving widowed bride and actually gained a fraction of sympathy from those who knew Thomas well, until they remembered they had never seen her before and that everyone knew they had only known each other for a few weeks before flying off to Vegas to get married.

After the funeral, Lydia and Mavis headed back to the house and skipped the reception that was held at Dunwoody Country Club. Lydia had packed up what she needed earlier that morning and she wanted to change and get her things. When they pulled back into the drive at the Reynolds house, there was already a realtor sign in the front yard and Lydia smiled when she rode past and saw it. You could almost see the canary feathers hanging from her mouth and her tail slowly whipping back and forth.

CHAPTER 26

Archer went home to look in on Jimmy and change his bandages; he had let Brody and Jane go to the funeral. He felt a little sad when he crossed the cattle guard and Jimmy didn't come shooting out from under the big oak.

Right then Mavis' cell phone rang again. She held it to her ear and said "Thanks," and tossed it aside.

"It's on," she said smiling as Lydia looked confused.

Archer punched in the alarm code and went inside, where he was greeted by Jimmy, who seemed to be getting his strength back. Jimmy got his training from the Department of Defense in Lackland Air Force Base, Texas. He was used to pain and exhaustion, but he was getting too old to retain the stamina he once had. Archer could tell Jimmy was feeling better today, and he was starting to feel a little better himself. Archer was sitting on the couch scratching Jimmy behind the ears when Jimmy gave a low growl and pointed to the big window. He took a 38 pistol from between the cushions and slid it in the fold of his arm sling. Archer looked out the big picture window and saw a utility truck coming down the driveway in a trail of dust. He had never seen a Walton EMC truck this far south in Rockdale County before. When the doorbell rang he could see through the side windows on the door that it was a stocky man with oily, dark hair and black eyes and he was wearing a tool belt with a radio clipped to it holding a clipboard and a pen. Archer opened the door partway and stopped, leaving his arm in the sling behind the door.

"Good afternoon, sir. Pardon me, but is this 33 Route 9 west?" he asked, smacking a piece of gum.

"No, this is not. Don't you have a phone number to that place on a work order or something?" Archer asked.

"Yeah, but when I called, no one answered. Say, would you mind looking at this map for me, maybe you can shed some light on where I am," he said, extending his clipboard.

Archer was locked on the man's eyes and said "That stuff will rot your teeth out, you know."

"Naw, it's got no sugar. It's gum to help me stop smoking," he said smiling. "My wife is making me quit."

Archer nodded and said "Sure. Let me see that map."

Then the man took his eyes off Archer for just a second to look at the clipboard he was handing to him – and that's when Archer grabbed his wrist and yanked him inside, spinning him around and jamming the 38 into his neck.

Archer gave the command, "Jimmy, secure!"

Jimmy latched onto his balls and clamped down just enough to immobilize him. Archer searched him and found a small 25 caliber, probably the one he shot Archer with, and a knife. Then he reached around to his back pocket and took out a wallet and noticed a Nazi swastika tattoo on his neck.

"Now, we're going to have a little chat," he said, opening the wallet. "Ryan Nichols, is it? When you don't give me the answer I want, Jimmy here is going to tighten down on your junk a little more each time you lie to me. You hearing me, Bubba?"

He nodded. He was sweating profusely and chomping away on the gum.

"I'm assuming Ryan Nichols is not your name," Archer said.

"It is, I don't know who you are but – owwww!" he screamed.

Archer had said, "Jimmy," and Jimmy clamped down a little harder.

"OK! OK!" It's Horace Macanelli. People call me Mac," he admitted.

"See, now that wasn't so hard, was it Horace?" Archer asked.

"Why are you here?"

"I was supposed to tie you up and sit you in front of a video cam and wait for orders."

"A video cam? For what? And orders from whom?" Archer asked.

"Yeah, a webcam and hook it up to my laptop, so it can be viewed remotely," Mac answered.

"Orders from whom?" Archer asked again in an irritated voice.

"I don't know, I never met her."

"Jimmy," Archer said.

"Owww! OK! OK! Make him stop. He's about to bite off my balls," Mac screamed as the veins in his neck protruded.

"Indeed he is. Now answer the question." Blood was starting to show through his work pants around Jimmy's mouth.

"Her name is Mavis, they call her Rooster. I swear, that's all I know about her. She calls me when she needs a job done. She's dialed in all over this state, she has friends everywhere. She does business by trading favors mostly."

"Like asking you to kill Dan and Peter West-brook?"

"Something like that – owww! Come on now!"

"And you killed Thomas Reynolds and shot me, too, didn't you?"

"Hey, that old man wasn't even supposed to be there, and you were chasing me," Mac said.

"Sorry I messed up your little killing spree. And how can you have a Nazi tattoo? You're Italian, you stupid fuck. Nazis hate you people too."

Archer saw a shimmer of reflection through the big window coming from the tree line. He could surmise it was the scope of a rifle. He'd seen enough to know what they looked like. Archer put another chair by the one he had Mac in.

"What's that for?" asked Mac.

"It's for your buddy out past the tree line," Archer replied.

You could see the regret in his eyes as he realized his only hope of rescue had been exposed.

He tied Mac to his chair and said to Jimmy, "Hold."

Jimmy let go off Mac's balls and sat inches in front of him growling.

Archer went out of the door on the north side

of the house and threw a saddle on Jesse and mounted. He circled back around behind the tree line on the south side and came down a game trail through the cypress. He saw a girl in a clear spot just behind the fence. He took a calving rope from the saddle and threw it around her just as she was turning to see what was behind her. He jerked back on the lasso hard and heard the air rush out of her lungs as she tried to say something. He was off of his horse and had her hogtied in a few seconds, and he did it all with one arm. He turned her over and was surprised to see that it was Keri Martin. He shook his head in disgust and threw her over the back of the horse and picked up her rifle and inspected it. It was a Belgian made Browning Automatic 7 mm. The kind of rifle used to bring down big game like bear and mountain ram. He didn't say a word to her on the way back to the house and she was cursing at him every step. When he reached the front porch, he pulled Keri off the horse and dropped her to the ground and again heard the air leave her lungs. He took the saddle off Jesse, put it on the steps, slipped off the bridle and reigns, slapped him on the backside, and gave a sharp whistle. The horse took off back to the stables, and Archer took Keri inside and tied her up next to Mac.

"Nice job, asshole," she said to Mac.

Archer shoved a dish rag in each of their mouths and used duct tape to seal it with.

CHAPTER 27

Archer went into his study and called Brody.

"Yeah, Boss."

"Hey there, Brother. I've got a couple of unfriendlies here at my house tied up," Archer said in a matter of fact sort of way.

He told Brody what had occurred since he got home and told him to email the rap sheet on Horace Macanelli and Keri Martin to him, then to come to the ranch, but to be stealthy because he wasn't sure who all was involved. Then he told Brody to call Jane and let her know what had happened and say that he would call her soon. He pressed Mac and Keri's fingers and thumbs on an inkpad from his study and imprinted them on a sheet of typing paper, then scanned it and sent it to Brody. A few minutes later he was reading the accomplishments of his new friends.

Keri had the usual juvenile arrests, shoplifting, drugs, and vandalism. The arrest report told the story of an angry little girl who had a problem with authority.

Mac was a different story. He read the report and went back in the front room. Mac and Keri were glaring at each other.

"Jimmy, secure," Archer ordered.

Jimmy looked back and forth between Mac and Keri then he looked back at Archer as if to say "Which one?"

"Him," Archer said nodding at Mac.

Jimmy immediately reattached his jaws to Mac's genitals in a swift snap.

Mac screamed in pain.

"Horace, you've been a bad boy in California, huh?" Archer said already knowing the answer.

Mac said nothing as he grit his teeth trying hard to conceal the pain.

"You have warrants all over that state, everything from murder to kidnapping. Shit, this time next week you'll be housed in Administrative Segregation in San Quentin, that is if Jimmy doesn't turn you into a girl first. Then you'll have to go to a women's facility. Yep, no Broadway block for you. Hey, maybe you'll be famous like some of the others from San Quentin. You'll be like Merle Haggard, Sirhan Sirhan or better yet, Stanley Tookie Williams. Say what you want about Tookie, he had focus. You think you'll make it as a Crip? Or will a fat, racist fuck like you join the Aryan Brotherhood?"

"And you, Keri," Archer said with disdain, feeling betrayed. "Is that why you doped me up that night, so you could find a spot on the property to take pot shots from and pull off this little hit you guy's cooked up? How did you get involved in all of this?" he asked and pulled the tape away from one side of her mouth

"I knew we were going to kill you the first night I met you at The Mug. The shot I took at your little whore was just for fun, that and I was bored"

"Who's we?"

"Me and my Mama and her friend."

"Who's your mama? Wait, let me guess. Mavis the Rooster," Archer asked.

"Her and her friend. Who you think's calling the shots, dumb shit? And when she finds out you got me here, she's gonna be coming for your ass."

"I'm counting on it," Archer said as he taped her mouth back shut. Archer knew her friend had to be Darla Davis Reynolds.

Archer got the camera gear out of the truck that Mac had stolen and took it inside and set it up in front of Mac and Keri and told Jimmy to keep an eye on them and left the room.

Jimmy released Mac again and took up his position in front of the two chairs staring at them.

CHAPTER 28

Archer quickly ran outside and jumped in his truck. He wanted to stay out of the open as much as he could. He drove to the front gap by the oak and got out. He looked around for a few seconds and picked up a newspaper in a plastic sock lying in the grass and threw it in the truck and returned back to the house. Jimmy always brought the paper in the house and dropped it in Archer's chair, but with Jimmy on sick leave, it was up to Archer for the time being.

He walked back in and found Mac lying on his side with Jimmy clamped down on his neck and Keri laughing through the duct tape.

"Let him go, Jim," Archer said and he raised Mac up, and situated him in the shot again. He took the newspaper out of the sock and laid it on the corner of the coffee table in plain view of the camera.

"OK, now you two play nice." He reached down and turned on the laptop, hit the 'record' button, turned on the live feed, then ran up to the panic room and turned on the wall of monitors and called Jane.

"Did Brody get a hold of you?" he asked.

"Yeah, I'm on my way."

"Look, make sure you go down to the end of my road and hide in the back pasture. Stay out of sight until you get a call on your cell phone. I set the trap, and I'm waiting on the rabbit."

"Archer, do you always have to talk like you're in an old black and white movie?"

"Yep," he said proudly.

"Archer?"

"Yeah?"

"Well…"

"Don't. You don't have to say anything. I know, and I think you're the cat's meow, too, Darling."

"OK, be careful."

Archer called his alarm company and told them they were expecting trouble at the ranch and that if the alarm goes off, they were to call Brody and Lieutenant Kincaid, and he left their numbers. He called Brody back.

"Where are you?"

"I just picked up Doc. Twenty minutes out."

"Got it. Do you have your laptop?" asked Archer.

"Of course."

"Go to our company Ethernet site and watch the video feed from the stables. You guys be ready for anything and wear your microphones and ear buds. Call Jane and give her our radio frequency and the website password so she has eyes and ears, too," Archer said as he clipped his microphone to his collar.

"Roger that. Brody out."

Archer rolled his eyes and put the cell phone in his pocket. He locked Mac's 25 caliber in his gun safe and grabbed his 45 off the wall and put on his Kevlar vest. He was watching the property and Mac and Keri from his desk in the panic room.

He was ready.

CHAPTER 29

Lydia received the email confirmation from the attorney that $390 million had been deposited at Chase. She and Mavis were floored when they found out how much the stock was actually worth. They went into the living room and Lydia poured them some champagne to celebrate, and Mavis pulled out her laptop and punched in an address. When the live video feed popped up, she could see Mac and Keri tied to chairs. Mac was still sweating and Keri had been crying and her mascara had run down her face until she looked like Alice Cooper.

"Fuck, Fuck, Fuck," Mavis screamed.

"What, baby. What is it?" Lydia asked.

Mavis turned the screen towards Lydia.

"Who are they?" asked Lydia.

"That is Mac," she said pointing at Mac. She

was furious. "And that is my daughter, Keri."

"Where are they?"

"Archer's house. Mac was supposed to have Archer tied up in that chair and we were going to send commands to Mac for what to do to Archer. Kind of like the Subservient Chicken, but more violent. It was supposed to be a gift for you, but it's obviously all fucked up now."

"You have a daughter? I never knew that."

"Yeah well, in my business you don't exactly go around advertising the fact that you have family; it's dangerous for them," Mavis admitted. "We have to go get Keri now and deal with Archer once and for all. We have to kill Mac, too," Mavis said.

"I don't care because he's a man and he's ex-pendable, but why Mac?" Lydia asked curiously.

"Because once he's arrested, it won't take long for the cops to figure out who hired him and that they have the wrong guy in jail. We have to rescue Keri and make it look like Mac and Archer killed each other. Then we can transfer the money to an offshore account, and, by this time tomorrow, we'll be sipping tiny little oriental drinks in Thailand where they have no extradition laws. Now let's go."

Brody dropped a couple of men off at the front gate by the big oak, a first line of defense, then he drove down the driveway and pulled his car into Archer's stable and closed the door. Doc took the high position in the loft by the window; he could see the driveway leading up to the house. If someone came by vehicle, they would have to come right into his line of sight.

It started to rain, and the sky was turning black. It wasn't one of those late afternoon summer showers that would be cleared up in thirty minutes; there was an ominous storm coming. Brody was in position under the awning on the back of the stable. He was covering the back of the house and couldn't help wondering if the storm on the rise was a metaphor for what was about to occur.

"Archer. We're in position and we have the front driveway and the back of the house in line of sight and video and we have two men at the front of the property with one standing order 'No one passes.' Please advise, over," Brody whispered into the microphone.

"Now we wait for the rabbits," Archer replied.

It was dark and raining hard when Mavis turned onto Archer's road. She stopped at the front of the driveway, backed up about a hundred yards short of his mailbox, and got out of the car. She followed the power line back with her eyes to the transformer box on the pole, raised the shotgun, and fired. It exploded in a shower of sparks, and she got back in the Lexus and drove another fifty yards and stopped again.

"You get out and go up this cut about three hundred yards, then cut over towards his house. You should be about even with it. Stop at the tree line and wait for my signal on your cell phone. I'll call you when it's safe to come in or if I need help, so be cautious on your approach. One more thing, if something happens to me promise you will look after Keri for me," Mavis ordered.

"OK, I promise. Good luck," she said as she chambered a round in her gun and kissed Mavis and got out.

"Boss, we lost the video feed and because of the rain we have zero visibility," Brody said into his collar. The generator kicked on, but it supplied only minimal lights and appliances.

"They cut the power, which means they're here. Stay sharp, fellas."

"Archer, I'm here too, but blind," said Jane.

"Remember, wait for the alarm company to call you, then move in," Archer said, and he went downstairs.

CHAPTER 30

Mavis started to turn into the long driveway and was stopped by two men. One man stopped in front of the car while the other approached the driver's side window. The guy in front of the car started talking into his sleeve just as the other man laid his palms on the inside window frame and lowered his head to look in. Mavis pulled the trigger of the shotgun she had pointed up from her lap and stomped on the accelerator at the same time. The top of the man's head peeled back and the sides sank inward until it looked like a deflated basketball. The other guy was plowed over, and then ground down in the cattle guard. She backed over him a second time to be sure he wouldn't come back and be a problem later. The last thing she needed was some last minute thing that could bite her on the ass because of sloppy work.

Mavis turned the headlights off and slowly crept down the driveway. She ditched the car and walked up to the house the last hundred yards staying on the side of the drive. When she got up to the big picture window, she could see Mac and Keri inside. Sheets of rain were pelting her. Then Archer passed in front of the window, and Mavis lifted her shotgun and fired. The shot bounced off of the window and Archer hit the deck and watched her through the window. Doc immediately shot where he saw the gun blast and hit Mavis in the chest. She spun around in a 360° in one flailing motion and fired haphazardly into the top window of the stable. A second later Doc fell out of the dark landing on the barbwire fence on his face. Half of his neck was missing and he was dead before he fell. Keri watched her mother fall to her knees trying to punch a number on her phone before she fell dead.

Keri started crying and Archer crawled to the east door and circled around to the front where Mavis lay.

"You must be Mavis. Glad to meet you," Archer said to the corpse while trying to catch his breath.

Then he was startled from behind "You piece of shit, Archer. Don't you move except to drop your gun and turn around real slow," Lydia said from behind him.

"OK, Darla, take it easy I'm doing it."

"Now let's go. Back in the house, real fucking slow."

When they went inside Lydia untied Mac and Keri and tied Archer down in the chair. Jimmy was no where in sight.

"Your boy just killed the only person I ever

cared about and you are gonna fucking pay for that," Lydia said

"And that was my mama, you dickless motherfucker. I ought to split your head open right now – and where's that fucking dog?" Keri said looking around.

Archer wanted to get her off the subject of Jimmy.

"Well, if your mama wasn't a homicidal maniac she wouldn't be dead right now. Look, I'm sorry you've had a bad time of it with your family, especially knowing how much you miss your little boy, Terry, since he died and all," Archer said trying to sound sympathetic.

"I never had no little boy. Terry wasn't no little boy. She was my mother, Mavis Teri McAvoy, and she wasn't dead until your man killed her. She was in prison."

"Mac, go look upstairs and try to find some candles and go in the kitchen and bring me the sharpest three knives in there and see if you can find a pair of pliers. I'm gonna give Archer the Lester Doyle treatment and skin him alive, except I won't use any drugs to knock him out. It'll be more fun that way," Lydia said looking at Archer.

Mac walked slowly away, bowlegged and grumbling something about his balls.

"Lydia?" Archer said squinting trying to get a closer look at her.

"Oh, thanks for catching up. You're a quick one, Archer. I told you I would get you one day for fucking me in court," Lydia said with a smirk.

"So, let's see if I got this right: you and that thing on my front sidewalk conjure up this lame-ass plan and hire bigfoot in there to kill the Westbrook Brothers and your husband to get their stock and you get away with all that money. It didn't occur to you that Mac was going to sell you out then we'd come after you? Man, are you stupid. I was wondering when you were going to surface. No wonder it took you so long to strike. You were healing from facial reconstruction, weren't you? It didn't work very well, you look kind of weird."

"Harlan was supposed to take the rap, and it got all fucked up when Mac couldn't seem to get the drop on you, but I did." Lydia said, and then she brought the 9 mm down on the side of Archer's head, and blood started dripping down on the carpet.

Lydia turned and stormed off in the direction of the kitchen, Keri in tow.

Jimmy came slowly out of the foyer and gave a slight whine as he licked the blood from the carpet and put his head in Archer's lap.

"There you are boy. Now go turn on the alarm Jimmy, the alarm," Archer said with his head swimming.

Jimmy turned and disappeared into the foyer and Archer could hear him pawing the keypad by the front door. He couldn't see him, but he saw the green light in the dark room turn red. It had an auxiliary battery and he could tell when Jimmy did it. Then Jimmy returned.

"Good boy, Jimmy, now go hide."

When Mac had gone into the kitchen, Brody was waiting behind the door. He hit Mac in the back of the neck with the butt of his gun, dragged him out of the kitchen door into the grass, and cuffed him to a water pipe on the side of the house.

CHAPTER 31

Lydia came barging through the door. "Mac, what the hell's taking you so long?"

Mac wasn't there.

"Keri, go find him," Lydia ordered, and Keri disappeared.

Lydia found a flashlight with a magnet on the handle stuck to side of the refrigerator. She found a long filet knife and a pair of pliers in a drawer and returned to Archer.

She didn't say a word as she walked in and laid her gun on the table, straddled Archer, and tore off his shirt.

"A bullet proof vest. You're such a pussy, Archer," Lydia said.

Then she said, "Why don't we start with your torso." She made a long cut from his pectoral muscle all the way down to his waist. Archer winced and gritted his teeth. Then she cut another one parallel to the first about three inches apart and she cut a flap at the top. She dropped the knife and clamped the pliers onto the flap and pulled down with all her weight. It stripped the length of skin off in one long piece. Archer groaned and threw his head back in pain. It felt like someone was pouring lava down his chest, but he would never let her know how much it hurt. From the corner of his eye he saw Jimmy, who came out of nowhere, flying through the air and landed on Lydia toppling her to the ground and clamped down on her neck. A few seconds later, Keri came rushing in the room and quickly grabbed Lydia's gun and pointed it at Jimmy.

"Drop that fucking gun or I'll air condition your head for you," Jane said stepping out of the south hallway.

"Shoot her, Jane! She's the one who shot at you and hurt Jimmy," Archer yelled.

"Lady, you have about one second to drop that gun, or I'm gonna put a hole in your face the size of a beer can. Now drop the fucking gun!" Jane demanded.

Keri's eyes darted back and forth between Jimmy, Lydia, and Jane. Then she swung the gun towards Jane and started to squeeze the trigger, and Jane shot her in the face. It blew Keri's nose off and left a huge hole right through her face between her eyes and her mouth. She dropped Lydia's gun and grabbed her face out of reflex and blood spider-webbed down both of her forearms as her eyes glassed over and she fell forward and landed flat on her face.

Brody came in from the kitchen and assessed the room. He went over to deal with Lydia, and Jane walked over to Archer and untied him.

"Heel, Jimmy. Why, you sneaky little bitch," Brody said as he cuffed Lydia, stood her up, and started walking her to the center of the room.

In what seemed like slow motion, Mac came smashing through the kitchen door swinging a section of the water pipe in circles over his head like a lasso. It was still cuffed to his arm and on about the third revolution, he crashed it into the side of Brody's head.

Out of reflex Archer snatched Jane's gun from her belt and pumped three rounds into Mac's heart. He crashed to the floor like a falling tree, and dust puffed up where he hit the carpet.

Jane grabbed a throw blanket from the back of the couch and a pillow and wrapped Brody's head in it and laid his head on the pillow.

"How is he? Is it bad?" Archer asked Jane.

"His head is split wide open and he looks like he's going into shock."

Archer grabbed the phone and directed 911 to respond.

Jane hugged Archer, which made him wince, then wiped the blood from his face and inventoried his injuries.

"How bad are you hurt?" she asked.

"I'm alright; it's just a scratch."

"Alright, I'll take her in and have her arrested and then I'll release Harlan. You go to the hospital with Brody and get patched up, and I'll meet you guys there later," Jane said to Archer.

She had radioed in for the troops when she got the call from the alarm company and there were cops pouring onto the property. She would make sure that the account holding all of the money went to Bobby Westbrook. She also took the huge wad of cash she got off Lydia's person at the time of her arrest and accidentally put it in Harlan's manila envelope in the property cage. Then she went upstairs to have Harlan released. She felt bad about Harlan. He had a rough enough life without being falsely accused and detained. Archer had been right about him and the accidental filing of her cash was the one chance she could give him. If he wanted a better life for himself he could do it now by making the right decisions. She processed him out and offered him a ride home.

Harlan opened up the envelope on the way home in Jane's car.

"I don't think this is mine," he said holding it open and showing her the money.

"I don't know what you're talking about, but if I had all that money I would get out of this neighborhood, get clean, and take care of my father. That's just what I would do," she said with a wink. "Harlan, most people go through life thinking that Easy Street is right around the corner. When in fact it's not. Easy Street is on top of a high mountain that you can see from a long way away. Every time you make a smart decision in life you get a little closer to it, but when you make a stupid one, you seem to fall back three spaces. My point is you're basically a good person, and I know you want out, but you can't get there waiting for the big score. You have to start off looking at what you want from a long way away. Get a job, pay taxes, and cut the grass, you follow? Then with clean living and making smart decisions you just might make it, or at least get close to it. The road leading to Easy Street, which isn't a bad place to be, is a hell of alot better than jail or death, and you get to sleep at night and don't always have to look over your shoulder. This is your chance to get a few steps closer to Easy Street, Harlan, or at least an access road. So make the right decisions for a while and see where it takes you," Jane said as she was pulling over to the curb.

Harlan shoved the money back in the envelope, and a tear started running down his cheek.

"Lieutenant, I promise on my mother's grave I'll do just what you said. I've wanted to clean up and get out of this place, but like you said, I needed the big score right around the corner. I'm going to put my father in the nursing home where they can take better care of him than I could. I have an Aunt in Chicago, and I can stay with her 'til I get a place of my own. I guess playing guitar for a living is better than selling drugs. There's a lot of blues clubs in Chicago, and I know some guys who came through here before that stay up there. I thank you for everything you done for me, but you won't see me 'round here no more."

He shook her hand and thanked her again profusely then he got out in front of his house, and, when Jane was pulling away, she looked in the rearview mirror and saw Harlan and his father, both sitting on the porch, waving.

CHAPTER 32

Three days later, Archer was released from the hospital and Jane picked him up.

"When does Brody get to go home?" she asked.

"Tomorrow. He had forty stitches and a concussion and they want to keep him another day for observation."

"I'm sorry about Doc; I know how much you cared about him."

"I just can't believe how lucky she got with that shot. She didn't even aim," Archer said shaking his head.

"Yeah, unfortunately good luck isn't only reserved for good people," she pointed out.

"Why don't we have that Chateau Briand dinner we never got to have, and you can nurse me back to health," he suggested.

"You've got a deal, Archer. And if you're a good patient, maybe I'll give you a sponge bath," she said with a naughty look on her face just as she turned into his driveway.

Jimmy shot out of nowhere, just as he always had, and dusted Jane to the house; unlike, Archer she couldn't bare not to let him win every time.

Alice Mae had cleaned and sanitized the whole place after the showdown and Archer felt like a sense of normalcy had been restored. He felt blessed to be alive and have his woman and his dog at home with him.

They enjoyed a wonderful dinner and made love listening to an entire Keb Mo CD. When they had finished and the CD ended, they lay with the windows open, breathing hard.

"Do you hear that?" asked Jane.

They listened closely.

On the wind, in the sliver of the silence, between the cicadas and crickets they could hear a pleasant and reassuring voice humming the tune, "Down by the Riverside."

About The Author

J.D. Bowen was born and raised in Georgia. He now has a home in Florida.

Hostile Takeover is the first in a series of novels featuring the daring exploits of Jon Archer. Be on the lookout for more in this exciting saga!

Made in the USA
Columbia, SC
05 January 2020